HOUSEBREAKER

HOUSEBREAKER

David Linzee

E. P. DUTTON NEW YORK

Publisher's Note: This novel is a work of fiction. Names, characters, places, and incidents either are the product of the author's imagination or are used fictitiously, and any resemblance to actual persons, living or dead, events, or locales is entirely coincidental.

Published in the United States by E. P. Dutton,
a division of NAL Penguin Inc.,
2 Park Avenue, New York, N.Y. 10016.

Library of Congress Cataloging-in-Publication Data

Linzee, David, 1952–
    Housebreaker.

    I. Title.
PS3562.I56H68   1987   813'.54   86-29318
ISBN 0-525-24523-5

OBE

DESIGNED BY EARL TIDWELL

1 2 3 4 5 6 7 8 9 10

First Edition

To my wife,
and to the memory of my mother

PART I

1

Her own apartment had no view, so Megan had not yet learned to take Paul's view for granted. She could not get used to having a pleasant prospect on offer whenever she cared to turn her head. She would stop what she was doing, perch on the sofa, and lose herself in gazing.

The sun had just come up; it was still so low in the sky that she could look at it directly. It was small, round, and shiny, like a new coin, and it seemed balanced on edge atop a tall tree on the far bank of the harbor. The trees were turning to russet and olive now, and the sugar maples stood out like match flames. But the foliage was still thick enough to hide from sight all but the chimneys and turrets of the old houses along the shore. The sun cast a streak of orange across the water, which was otherwise as still and blue as the cloudless sky. A small boat was setting sail from the marina just below the window. The man at the tiller was the only human being in sight.

Paul always got the pick of everything: his apartment was in the farthest building, so that the rest of the condominium complex, and the six-lane turnpike that ran by it, were invisible. But he could do nothing about the railroad bridge that barred the mouth of the harbor from the sea. Even as she watched, a commuter train bound for the city shot out of the woods on the far shore and ran across the bridge. She could hear the purposeful rumble and clatter of its wheels through the heavy glass of the window.

Behind her the parquetry creaked under Paul's footsteps. He must have been awakened by her absence from his side. He sank down behind the sofa and rested his head against hers. In a voice husky with sleep he said, "What are you doing up?"

She had to think for a moment. That was the problem with an entire weekend of doing just as you pleased: your purposes, newly formed, kept slipping away. "I was going to make some coffee and bring it up to you. I used to do that for my father. He said the aroma of coffee was about the least objectionable thing you could wake up to on a Monday morning."

"Oh. I forgot it was Monday." He struggled to his feet. "When you don't have to come back from somewhere, it sort of sneaks up on you."

She nodded. It was the first time they'd had a whole weekend together and not gone away. They had not left the apartment at all; Paul hadn't even walked downstairs to get the mail or opened the door to pick up the newspaper. When the doorbell rang, or somebody yelled out his name from the path below the balcony, they'd held still, grinning, like children playing hide and seek. The telephone was hooked to an answering machine, which he had adjusted so that they heard neither the ring nor the voices. Its red light had glared at them, to tell them it was full of messages, until Paul had dropped a towel over it.

Megan slid back against the arm of the sofa. The nubby fabric rubbed against her bottom and she realized that she had nothing on. She hadn't even thought of putting on a robe when she got out of bed. Just as she was always going out into these

4

chilly October days without a coat, having lost the habit of coats over the summer, she seemed, over this weekend, to have lost the habit of wearing any clothes at all.

Paul was naked too. She watched him as he locked his hands behind his neck and arched his back, stretching. His body was as familiar to her, and as pleasing to look at, as his face.

He caught her eye, and held it for a moment. Then he leaned toward her. He kissed her forehead, and the tip of her nose, and her mouth. His chin was rough with stubble, his tongue warm and active. That familiar mood blended of languor and urgency was taking hold of Megan already—her thoughts were slipping away. It happened to her very quickly these days.

She was sliding her arms around him when the faint, insistent buzz of the alarm clock reached her from upstairs. It got into her head, and her thoughts started up again.

"We could ignore it," he suggested.

"We can't. I set it as late as I dared."

She patted his arm and turned away. The boat she had noticed before was passing beneath the bridge to open water. Paul had a boat, too, moored in the marina below the window. She said, "I wish we'd gone for a sail. There probably won't be any more nice weekends."

"Oh, I don't know. Too many people out there."

When Paul said that a coldness seemed to touch her skin. She remembered now that of course they could not go for a sail. When he did take her out in the boat, they would have to get an early start, and he would be in a hurry to stow the gear and rig the boat before anyone he knew came along.

Suddenly the faint buzz of the alarm clock was insufferably irritating. She felt embarrassed by her nakedness; she sat upright and folded her arms.

Paul was on his way to the kitchen. He called out, "I'll bring the coffee upstairs, okay?"

She did not reply. Going up to the bedroom she shut off the nagging alarm. As she took a quick shower and began to dress, her nettlesome thoughts only grew worse. Soon she was pacing the room in her slip, taking deep breaths, and trying to compose herself before Paul came up. It was her own fault for mentioning the sailboat. She would not let that spoil the weekend.

5

Paul came in with the coffee cups. He was wearing only his bathrobe: he could read the paper and dress leisurely, and drift into the office at nine thirty or ten. She had to be at her desk by eight thirty sharp.

She put the thought away, forced a smile, and thanked him for the coffee. Then she went on with her dressing.

"Anything the matter, Meg?"

"No. Everything's fine."

"Well, okay." He started to turn away, but instead leaned back against the doorjamb. "You know, it seems like all our arguments take place inside your head. By the time I figure out you're mad at me, it's all over. I feel kind of left out."

Despite herself Megan smiled. "I'm not mad at you. And I'm no good at arguing."

"Okay, we won't argue. Just tell me what's bothering you."

"It's just that—all along I've been thinking how nice it was to have the weekend to ourselves. But it's not so nice when you remember that we're in hiding from other people. That whenever we're together, we have to be alone together."

He shrugged. "I don't want to be bothered with them. I thought you felt the same."

"I did at first. But the precautions are starting to get to me."

"Okay. What do you want us to do?"

"Just not to be so—so careful all the time. To go out in public like anyone else."

Paul straightened up and folded his arms. "Okay. We can do that. And if we do, people in the firm are going to hear about us. Talk about us. Are you ready for that?"

She turned away, to take a blouse out of the closet. "I don't see why they have to. It's not as if we're committing a crime or something. There's no rule against dating in the firm."

"No. But they'll talk anyway."

"Because you're a lawyer and I'm not." Megan was doing up the buttons, and kept her eyes on them.

"Oh, they'd talk about us no matter who we were. Though that certainly doesn't help. I mean—can you imagine what the other paralegals will say?"

Megan did not answer for a moment. She walked back to the closet and knelt to look for a pair of shoes. Paul waited.

Finally she said, "I can. I have. That's why I tried to keep this argument to myself."

"I'm sorry, Meg. This isn't—isn't permanent, you know." Paul seemed to want to say more, but nothing came to him. She heard his footsteps going away, then the hiss of the shower. They never kissed good-bye in the morning. It made them both feel foolish, for in a couple of hours they would be meeting in some corridor of the firm and wishing each other good morning.

2

In midafternoon Megan was returning to the firm from an errand. She opened the heavy door marked GOLDMAN LASCH O'HARA TOWER & SWALES, and stepped into the reception lobby. She paused there for a moment, taking off her coat and waiting for her eyes to adjust to the darkness. The lobby was all heavy wood paneling and gray stone facings, a place of almost ecclesiastical gloom and hush. The office noises were shut away in back, so that you heard only the voice of the switchboard operator incanting, "Good afternoon Goldman Lasch . . . thank you one moment please." There were no windows to the outside to reveal that this was really an office suite in a glass-walled skyscraper in downtown Stamford. There were only long, narrow windows inset in one of the paneled walls which, like the chancel screens in old churches, both displayed and obscured the sacred mystery within: the library with

7

its serried ranks of tomes and its long tables, at which the lawyers sat, heads bowed over their yellow pads. All of them had their suit jackets on. This was in obedience to a library rule. Goldman Lasch was neither a large nor a venerable firm—all its name partners were still alive—but it was a very stuffy one.

She crossed the lobby and went through into the brightness and racket of the corridor. Paul's office door was open. It was just as well for the firm's image that he seldom worked in the library. His desk was covered with papers, and there was a barricade of file folders and books around his chair. He had his coat off, and his feet were propped on a filing cabinet. They were shod in brown penny loafers. Paul would frequently wear casual shoes, or a sweater instead of a vest, as if he meant to sabotage the somber correctness of his suits.

Catching sight of her, he grinned. "Hi."

"Hi. If you can give me the Berman file, I'll draft that motion you were wanting."

"Great. Thanks." He swung his feet down and started to sift through the folders on the floor.

Megan sat down in the chair beside the desk. It would take him a while to find the file, and then he would want to talk about something else before he told her what to do with it. Paul had always preferred chatting to work. That was how they had gotten to know one another.

At first she had assumed that she was there only to listen to his opinions and to laugh at his jokes. He was a partner, and that was what the other partners—those who had any time for her at all—expected. But it turned out that Paul Wyler actually had wanted to converse with her. He was an ardent weekend outdoorsman, and when he learned that she had grown up in deepest New Hampshire he had begun to question her about songbirds and wildflowers. Gradually the conversations grew more personal. Megan's father had been a Latin teacher at a boarding school with a moderately famous name, and Paul seemed to find her background quaint and intriguing.

That was as far as it went, for a very long time. For a span of several months, Paul was simply her favorite lawyer to work for. But sometime in the summer she noticed that when they passed in the hall, he was turning to glance after her. It became a habit for him to drop in on her at the end of the day, and sit and talk, stretching out his long legs until they touched the wall of her narrow office. His eyes would fix upon her, and there was a smile on his face that he did not seem aware of. Megan was not inexperienced with men, and she knew that it was time to give serious thought to the question of whether she should date someone she worked for, much less a partner. She decided that it wouldn't be wise, and worked out a polite refusal in her mind. But when the moment came to deliver it, she realized that she was going to hurt his feelings badly—and her own, too. She did not refuse.

"Berman. Here it is." He put the file unopened on his desk, as usual, and leaned back in his chair. "I've been wondering, Meg."

"What?"

"Have you given any more thought to your plans?"

"Plans," she said. He would ask about her plans from time to time, and Megan suspected that he was thinking that if she would only stop being a paralegal, their problem would go away.

"Yeah. Ever think about going back to your studies?"

"No. I've lost my taste for grad school. Nothing I like to study, nothing I'm good at, has a job waiting at the end of it. So I just wind up with bigger debts."

Paul nodded. "Yeah. Same here."

"I'm missing something."

"The only things I'm good at are camping out and watching baseball games on TV, and nobody would pay me to do either one. Maybe you ought to do what I did. And thousands like me."

"You mean go to law school? I never thought I'd hear you recommend that to anyone."

"It's all in pacing yourself. You suffer through the first year of law school, then you can coast through the rest of it. You go to a firm and suffer a few more years, and then you can coast forever."

"Oh, Paul, you don't coast. You work and worry. Anyway I had the feeling that you were . . . disappointed in the law."

"Disappointed? Why?"

"Well, because you started out as a Legal Aid lawyer, and you ended up—you know, here."

"Oh, you mean disappointed in my quest to establish justice in the land. Meg, the only disappointment you have to face when you become a lawyer is that the moral issues you keep expecting never turn up. I used to strive to lessen the punishment of the guilty. Now I strive to lessen the taxation of the wealthy. That's all."

"Well, then, I'm not as strong as you. I couldn't keep at something I didn't believe in."

Paul looked amused, his gaze intensified by his air of giving more weight to what she said than she'd intended. "Are you sure *strong* is the word you're looking for?"

They were interrupted—as they often were—by the telephone. Megan did not wait. She took the file from the desk and went out. These conversations with Paul made her feel restless and dissatisfied. It got worse once she was alone in her office, a doorless, windowless, cramped alcove at the end of the hall. She opened the file, and tried to bring her mind to bear on the business issues at hand.

Megan was a probate paralegal; she worked in the department of the firm called Trusts and Estates. After death a person enjoys a brief reincarnation as an estate, lasting until his debts are discharged, his taxes paid, and his worldly goods distributed. This was a drawn-out bureaucratic process, entirely devoid of ceremony. Even "the reading of the will," that staple of melodrama, rarely occurred in real life. Under the direction of the executor, usually Paul, Megan handled the estate's paperwork. Her job came down to paying bills, corresponding with banks and brokers, filling out tax and insurance forms, and proofreading the smallest of small print in documents. In other words, she handled the sort of legal technicalities that were so arid and exacting that even lawyers did not want to deal with them.

There were, broadly speaking, two kinds of paralegals. First, there were the dilettantes, who were putting in a year or so in the real world between college and graduate school. Then there were the serious paralegals, who had worked their way up from being secretaries, or earned degrees from paralegal institutes. They looked upon their jobs as careers and took pride in them. Megan had been at the firm too long to fit into the first group any more, and she was overqualified for the second. There were times when her situation would remind her of the plight of the governess in a Victorian novel. She was caught "between stairs"; neither the masters nor the servants considered her one of their own. And Megan had made the mistake of which those governesses were so afraid: she had lost her virtue.

She was just beginning to concentrate on the task at hand when the telephone rang.

"Megan Lofting."

"Yeah, Meg," the receptionist said. "I've got this client on the line who wants to talk to Mr. Wyler, and he's not there. Can you take her?"

"But he was just in his office."

"He's gone out. Will you take her?"

"Who is it?"

"I don't know. She doesn't want to leave a message, she wants to talk to somebody. Will you take her?"

"Yes, all right," said Megan, and in a moment the call came through. "Hello, can I help you?"

"Are you Paul's girl?"

"I beg your pardon?"

"Are you Paul Wyler's secretary?"

"Oh. No, I'm his legal assistant, Megan Lofting."

"Oh, of course. Megan. Hi, this is Barb Elkin."

Megan drew herself up. Mrs. Elkin—or rather, the estate of her late husband—was Paul's most important client. "I'm sorry, but Paul isn't available just now. Is there anything I can help you with?"

Mrs. Elkin paused to consider. There seemed to be a great commotion going on around her; Megan could hear a television playing and children laughing. "We can't deal with this over the phone anyway. You'll just have to get him over here. Can you do that for me?"

Megan hesitated. She dreaded situations like this. She had no authority to commit a lawyer to anything, yet she could not offend a client. "May I give him an idea what this is about?"

"It's this will, you see. I'm a little worried that Paul made a mistake."

Unconsciously she had dropped her voice so that Megan could hardly hear her above the background din. "A mistake? You mean a mistake in your will, Mrs. Elkin?"

"No. In Hal's. In my late husband's. It's not a big mistake, but I do want to get it straightened out."

Megan's heart took a long bound. You could not straighten out mistakes in a will once the testator was dead. Mrs. Elkin must be confused. Or at least Megan hoped that she was. She said carefully, "I'm sure Paul will want to discuss this with you as soon as possible. I'll have him call you."

"Oh no, just have him come over," Mrs. Elkin replied, as if she were making things easier for Megan. "Say five thirty or so."

"But Mrs. Elkin—"

She got no further, for the children's voices in the background had risen in a chorus of protest. It was a few moments before Mrs. Elkin got back to her. "We'll have to make that four thirty."

"But Paul isn't even here. He's—"

Mrs. Elkin rolled brightly over her. "I'm sorry, but I promised to take the kids to the mall for dinner. It'll have to be four thirty. Okay? Thank you, Megan. Bye-bye."

The line went dead.

Megan replaced the receiver and glanced at her watch: it was four o'clock already. She went hurriedly up the hall to Paul's office. It was empty.

"He's not back yet."

Paul's secretary Pamela was gazing coolly at her across the hall. She was a beautiful, sullen girl, not inclined to put herself out for paralegals. She was typing from a dictation cassette, and she did not pause or take off her headset.

"Did he say when—"

"He said about four." Pamela's heavily shadowed eyelids dropped like blue curtains as she returned her attention to her work.

Paul was usually prompt, and in any case there was nothing she could do but wait. She returned to her office and bent over the filing cabinet to pull out the hefty folder marked Elkin. The "Last Will and Testament" of Harold B. Elkin, a thick, blue-backed document, was on top. Megan put it in her lap and shifted her chair so that she could keep watch on the corridor. Idly she began to flip through the pages.

Surely there couldn't be anything wrong with it: the late

12

Mr. Elkin had taken so much care. If he was a fair example, the wealthy did not pass away as others did. Megan's father had lost all interest in his earthly possessions well before he went into the hospital for the last time. Mr. Elkin was different. The blow fate had dealt him by cutting short his life when he was just sixty-four had only made him more determined to see that he would not be cheated of having his way with the people and things he was leaving behind. Paul had spent much of May and June at the hospital, waiting for Mr. Elkin to be lucid enough to badger him about some detail or other. He'd been a demanding client right to the end, and surely there could be nothing in this will that was not just as he had wanted it.

She knew that was what Paul was going to say. He would tell her Mrs. Elkin was just being difficult and he was going to be very irritated with her for committing him to the appointment.

Looking up, she was just in time to see Paul go into his office. She took a deep breath, grasped the file, and got up.

He grinned happily as she came in, but Megan was too flustered to break the news gently. "Paul, something's happened," she blurted out. "You're going to have to go to Mrs. Elkin's right away. I'm sorry."

He did not reply at once, but his features reformed into a characteristic expression of amusement tinged with displeasure. He was wearing his horn-rimmed glasses, and, for reasons Megan could never figure out, these made the look even harder to bear. He said, "Why?"

"She's been reading the will and she found something she didn't like. She wants you to change it. Her husband's will, I mean."

"Her *husband's* will?" Paul leaned back in his chair and folded his hands behind his head. "Call her back. Tell her I can't help her. She needs a medium, not a lawyer. She's going to have to hold a séance and commune with Hal's spirit."

Megan smiled weakly. She had the feeling that once Paul had indulged his wit, he really was going to make her call Mrs. Elkin back and say she'd been unable to find him. "I'm really sorry," she said again. "I tried to put her off, but I couldn't handle her."

"Oh, I know the feeling." He continued to gaze upward

for a while. "She's a nice lady, really, and I'd probably like her if I weren't her lawyer. But . . . You know, Meg, there are two kinds of bad clients. The kind who can't understand anything you explain to them, and the kind who think they know better than you do. Barb Elkin's both. She makes me feel like one of her kids. 'Billy, you left your bike out in the rain. Paul, you made a mistake in the will. Neither of you will get any dessert tonight."

"You don't think it's possible that there really could be a mistake, do you?"

"I think it's rather unlikely," he replied, in a caustic tone. But even as he spoke he was glancing at his watch and getting up.

"You're going then, aren't you?" she asked hopefully.

"Always glad to be of service." He glanced at the heavy file cradled in her arms. "You got the latest set of valuations in there?"

"Yes, I do."

"Good. Might as well bring those as long as I'm going. You come too."

"Me?"

"Sure. You know a lot more about the valuations than I do." But he was looking mischievous as he turned away to pick up his briefcase.

"Paul, you're not doing this to punish me for sticking you with the appointment, are you?"

They exchanged one of those grins which, had it been seen by anyone in the firm, would have betrayed their intimacy more irretrievably than an embrace.

"Punish you? Of course not. What ingratitude! You're always complaining about how dull it is to be a paralegal, and here I'm offering you the chance not only to get out of the office early, but to call upon my richest client in her gracious residence on Shady Lane."

3

This is the genuine, original Shady Lane, Megan thought, as they turned into Mrs. Elkin's street. When a developer named some bleak street of saplings and split-levels in a new subdivision Shady Lane, he was trying to evoke visions of a place like this. They drove along between rows of tall old oaks and elms, whose weary October greenery formed a canopy far above the sun-speckled road. At the end of this verdant tunnel, beyond the fence and the private beach, the sea gleamed and beckoned. Well back across broad lawns, screened by boskage, stood the handsome, spacious houses.

"That's it," Paul said, pointing through the windshield, and as they drew nearer, the Elkin house emerged from its trees and hedges. It was a fine old place, partly stone and partly shingle, with wide verandas and a steep gabled roof crowned by a turret that would offer a splendid view of the sea.

It was the sort of house in which one could imagine a family living for generation upon generation. But that was not the case. Hal Elkin had bought the place only fifteen years ago; the current marriage, in fact, was itself only fifteen years old. Harold Elkin's first wife had died, and he had married a woman more than twenty years younger than he, and started a new family. These bare facts were about all that Megan knew of their lives. It was a peculiarity of her position that while she was on intimate terms with the Elkins' money, she was hardly acquainted with the people themselves. She had never met any of the Elkins, only corresponded with them or talked to them on the telephone. And the only one whom she spoke to regularly was Brian, Mr. Elkin's son by his first marriage. Brian tended to get into the sort of tangles with banks and insurance companies that it was her job to straighten out, and Paul tended to neglect to return his calls. She was not likely to see Brian today, though. He lived in the city, and she had the impression that he seldom came to Shady Lane.

Paul parked at the curb, as the driveway was blocked by a station wagon. A group of boys in slinky black wetsuits were busy lashing a sailboard to its roof.

"Are any of those Elkins?" Megan inquired as they got out of the car.

"No. This place is always crawling with kids, and surprisingly few of them turn out to be Elkins."

He was growing more irritable as the meeting with the client neared, so she did not ask him any more questions. He was right about the kids, though. On the tennis court by the side of the house, four boys hardly taller than their rackets were walloping two-handed drives while keeping up a braying commentary, television announcer style, each on his own prowess. Paul led the way up the steps and knocked on the back door. As they waited, a trio of little girls came thumping and giggling past, once, and then again. They were doing laps round the house on the verandas. They paid no attention to the grown-up visitors, and Paul did not glance at them.

The door was opened by a solemn-faced teenager in a neat print dress, who called Paul "sir," and stepped back, holding the door, with eyes downcast. This, Megan realized, was the one Paul called "the Mormon au pair." Mrs. Elkin, like a lot of Fairfield County matrons, would not entrust her children to the depraved local teenagers, and had imported a governess from Utah.

They stepped into the kitchen. It was a cavernous room, for the house had been built in an era when multitudes of servants labored over complicated banquets. Now it held paired sinks and dishwashers and fridges, and there was still room left over for a big table by a window. Here, among lists, color-

16

ing books, and toys, Barbara Elkin sat talking on the telephone. She smiled and waved her free hand.

It was a nice smile, for she had merry bright blue eyes and becoming wrinkles. She had on a polo shirt and baggy shorts. Her limbs were tanned and slender. Her graying light brown hair was drawn back, rather girlishly, into a simple knot. Diamonds glittered on her fingers as she hung the phone on the wall and came toward them.

"You must be Megan. Thanks so much for getting him over here." As she spoke she gripped Paul by the shoulders and elicited from him a kiss on the cheek. "Let's try to find a quiet nook, shall we? Come along."

She led them up the hall to a vast, rather gloomy living room. There were big plump sofas, and easy chairs attended by ottomans. A grand piano, heavily laden with family photographs, angled across the far end of the room. The Persian carpets were thick and resilient; walking upon them was like crossing a golf green on a dewy morning. Breakfront cabinets loomed up against the walls. They were full of little bits of crystal and porcelain. Megan had been astonished to learn from the valuations how much these bibelots were worth. In fact, she knew the value and provenance of everything in the room. It was interesting to be here, like visiting some exotic city she'd only read about in books. She anticipated a leisurely survey of the room while Paul and Mrs. Elkin talked. Since they would be discussing an important legal question, she would not be expected to contribute.

"Well, do sit down," said Mrs. Elkin, perching on the edge of a sofa, before a coffee table that was covered with papers, books, and a copy of the will. "Megan, try that wing chair, why don't you? Oh no, Paul, not there."

"This is fine."

"You're going to be looking at papers, you'll ruin your eyes. Sit over here."

Paul complied grudgingly. Mrs. Elkin took a cigarette from a silver case and lit it from a matching lighter, peering through the mullioned window and the rhododendron leaves outside it as she did so. "You wouldn't believe what a hard time the children give me if they catch me smoking. But I'm in a tizzy about this."

17

"I understand you've been reading the will."

"Yes. You know, I never did before. Just seeing 'Last Will and Testament' would make me go all weepy, and by the time I got to the specific bequests—" She broke off and made a brusque gesture with her cigarette. "But this morning I decided it was time I got on with it, so I got myself a bunch of those 'law for the layman' books, and a bottle of aspirin, and pitched in. And I found this mistake on the next-to-last page."

She picked up her copy of the will and put on her glasses. On cue, Megan took the file copy from her briefcase. But Paul did not ask her for it. He merely said, "Just what is the mistake, Barb?"

"It's this business about you having the authority to make payments from the trust directly to the children. Of course it doesn't matter now, when they're so young, but it could cause trouble a few years down the road. I remember talking it all over with Hal, and I know this isn't the way he wanted it. You've made a mistake, Paul, and you're simply going to have to fix it up. Now, before it causes any problems."

Megan suppressed a smile. This was why Paul dreaded dealing with Mrs. Elkin. She didn't actually shake her finger at him, but she seemed quite capable of doing so.

Paul said, in a neutral lawyer's tone, "Which trust is this?"

"The residuary trust, of course. That's the one where all our money is, isn't it?"

"Oh. The residuary trust." He sighed heavily. "Barb, you can set your mind at rest. I won't be making any payments to the children from the residuary trust. The language of the will expressly forbids it. It has to."

Mrs. Elkin looked up at him. Her eyes seemed larger behind the glasses. "It has to?"

"Yes. There would be a tax problem if it didn't. You see, under the federal estate tax law, assets that pass from husband to wife are not taxed. But assets that pass from parent to child *are* taxed. So if we had given your children access to the residuary trust, we would have incurred a whopping tax liability. That's why we didn't do it that way. If you'll recall, we discussed this at length while Hal was alive."

Mrs. Elkin was still peering at him. Unnoticed, the ash

18

dropped from her cigarette to the Persian rug. "Oh yes," she said, in a new, tentative voice. "Yes, I do remember something about that."

"Good," Paul said. He turned to Megan, his eyebrows raised in amusement. But out of the corner of her eye she could see Mrs. Elkin hunching over the will, her forefinger moving over the lines of type. It came to a stop. "So what does 'issue' mean, Paul?"

"Issue?"

"Yes. Isn't that what you lawyers say when you mean children?"

"That's correct."

"Well, I don't get it, then. It says here"—she began to read, beating time with her finger as she struggled over the convoluted legal syntax—" 'I give, devise, and bequeath my residuary estate to the fiduciary of the residuary trust, in trust, in the exercise of his absolute discretion, either colon numeral one, to pay so much of the net income thereof to or among any of my spouse and issue living . . .' "

Megan saw it at once. She saw that Mrs. Elkin had been right, and Paul wrong. The will contained a terrible mistake. Her insides crumpled up like a wadded ball of paper. She looked wildly at Paul.

His expression had not changed; he had not caught on yet. "No, Mrs. Elkin. It doesn't say 'and issue.' Just 'to my spouse.' "

Mrs. Elkin's finger moved back up the page. "But it does say 'and issue.' "

"No. You must have the wrong document there. It must be a draft of your will. That's where it talks about issue."

Mrs. Elkin flipped over to the signature page. "No, this is Hal's will. Really, Paul, you don't think I've been studying the wrong—"

Paul sprang to his feet and leaned across the table. "Uh—excuse me," he said, and took the will from Mrs. Elkin's hand. His face was as immobile as a mask, only his eyes moving back and forth as he read. He seemed stunned, as if the letters were breaking up and reforming before his eyes. He dropped the will on the table and picked up the file copy from Megan's lap.

There was another long silence as he read the sentence again. Then he sank down in his chair. His face was flushed and his hand trembled slightly.

"This will have to be fixed," he said at last.

"Well, that's what I've been saying all along." Mrs. Elkin glanced at Megan, in search of reassurance. "Really, Paul, you shouldn't give us such a fright."

Megan said to him gently, "What will we have to do to change it, Paul?"

"Well, I've never been in this situation before. . . . Uh, a will construction hearing. Yes. I have to go before a judge of the probate court, explain that this is an error, and get an order allowing me to correct it."

"I can't say I like this idea of going before a judge." Mrs. Elkin picked up the will and peered at it, as if scrutinizing a crooked hemline in the mirror. "It's only a couple of words. Couldn't we leave it?"

He made a dry, soughing sound that bore little relation to a laugh. "Try to slip it by, you mean? We could, but it would be bad news if the IRS caught it."

Mrs. Elkin flinched. "The IRS? What have they got to do with this?"

"Nothing," Paul said, hastily. "We'll get the will corrected before we have to file the estate tax return, and there'll be no problem. Really."

"Wait a minute." She leaned forward and crushed her cigarette into the ashtray. In the first moment all of them had been dazed and fumbling, but she was beginning to work it out now. "What you said before, about assets passing to the children being taxable, that doesn't mean that the whole residuary trust is taxable. Does it?"

"We'll get the language corrected, and it won't be taxable."

Mrs. Elkin shut her eyes and said, "How much tax?"

"Once we get it corrected—"

"How much tax?"

Paul said miserably, "Well, Barb, you're in the fifty-percent bracket."

Mrs. Elkin threw her head back and opened her mouth as if she could not get enough air. "This can't be," she said brokenly. "Half. Half of all the money we have in the world, because of a couple of words that shouldn't be here? Paul, how could you let this happen?"

Paul could think of nothing to say. He looked helplessly at Megan.

Megan said, "I'm sorry."

Mrs. Elkin turned to look at her. Her blue eyes were fierce with worry. "What do you mean, *you're* sorry?"

"I . . . I think I know how it happened. You see, in our office, nobody writes the wills, exactly. They're generated by word-processing machines. I've got this sort of a multiple choice form, with all the possible clauses on it, and Paul tells me which ones he wants in a particular will, and I check them off on the form and send it down . . . and the will comes back complete. This time I must have checked the box for the wrong kind of residuary clause. I—"

Mrs. Elkin turned her face away and put up her hand to make Megan stop. "Oh, I can't understand any of this! Paul, what's she talking about?"

Paul got to his feet. He stood with his hands in his pockets, waiting until she looked up at him. Then he said: "All Megan means is that this is a clerical error. We'll tell that to the judge. He'll say we can change it, and there will be no tax problem. You won't lose a penny, Barb."

By sheer force of will he had gotten that calm certainty back into his voice, and it had the desired effect. Mrs. Elkin gazed up at him a while longer. Then, slowly, her head began to nod.

"All right. You're sure about that?"

"I'm sure."

"Still, I don't want this hanging over me. Can't you tell the judge to do it right away?"

"Lawyers can't tell judges . . ." He smiled and began again. "I'll have a word with the clerk of court. Get us on calendar as soon as possible."

"Well, call and let me know." She put the will back on the table and pushed it away. "Oh, dear. I don't know who's going to take the children to the mall tonight."

"It'll be okay, Barb. But I think you're entitled to another cigarette."

Mrs. Elkin was smiling now, and Paul shot Megan a quick glance, to tell her that this was the time to leave.

He made no effort to keep up the front once they were alone. They drove back downtown in absolute silence. It was rush hour now, and the traffic was thick. They got into a jam underneath the turnpike. When they had not moved for several minutes, Paul took his hands off the wheel and bowed his head. He still did not say anything, but she could sense his wretchedness.

"Oh, Paul, I'm so sorry. If I'd been more careful when I checked those boxes—"

"Oh, that. Forget it. Maybe it wasn't your mistake at all, maybe it was Pam, or somebody in the word-processing center. We'll never know. Anyway, I should have caught it when I proofread. I'm responsible."

"Or I should. But all that boilerplate stuff, you see it so many times that you can't read it anymore. Your eye skims right over it—"

"Nicely put. I'll have to remember that when I go before the judge."

"There won't be any problem with the hearing, will there? I mean, they'll believe that it's just a mistake?"

"I expect so. It's too stupid to be anything but a mistake. So all I have to do is convince the judge of what an incompetent I am, and everything will be fine."

"Oh, Paul, don't. It's such an easy thing to miss. Like Mrs. Elkin said, just a couple of words."

She laid her hand on his arm, but he did not respond. There was another heavy silence. The car ahead of them moved forward a few yards, and the car behind honked. Paul closed the gap. They went on waiting.

"Maybe that's where I blew it," he said suddenly.

"What?"

"When Barb said it was just a small mistake and we ought to leave it. And I had to open my stupid mouth and tell her how much money she could lose. Christ. Not only am I incompetent, I let the client *know* I'm incompetent. I should've jollied her along, let the will go through as is, and hoped the IRS wouldn't catch the slip. Maybe it's not too late. Maybe I should call her tomorrow, say it was all a misunderstanding and everything's fine. Then sit back and pray." He turned toward her for the first time. "What do you think?"

"I . . . I don't know."

"What do you mean, you don't know? It's a simple choice. What should I do?"

She could feel his frustration coming to bear on her, and it rattled her badly. "Oh, Paul, don't ask me. You know what to do."

"No, I don't. I'm incompetent, remember?"

He kept on staring at her until she had to look away. "You're not incompetent, Paul. I'm sure . . . I'm sure that whatever you do will be right."

"Thanks. That's a real contribution to the debate. That really takes a load off my back."

A space opened in front of them, and Paul wrenched the wheel right and stepped on the gas. They were not going home. After a moment he turned again, into the garage entrance of the Goldman Lasch building, and drew to a stop behind her parked car.

"You go on home. I have to stop by the office for a while. Look up some cases and dig out the old drafts of the will."

"Can I help?"

"No. You go on home."

He was staring straight ahead, and Megan knew there was no point in saying anything more. She got out of the car, shut the door, and watched him drive away, to his privileged partner's space on an upper level.

4

The next morning Megan woke early from a fitful sleep. She was alone in the big bed. Paul hadn't come home at all. She dressed quickly and went to work. The corridors were very quiet in the slanting sunshine; hardly anyone arrived so early. She found Paul in his office.

The room was as messy as she had ever seen it, with crooked towers of books rising from the floor, and papers heaped on the sofa and chairs. But Paul, seated at his desk, smiled and wished her a cheerful good morning.

"You look . . . okay," she said.

"I managed to borrow a razor and a shirt. The associates are equipped for this all-night stuff. I'll be okay if nobody looks at my eyes too closely." He hesitated, then went on, "Did you sleep well? I hope I didn't upset you last night."

This was as close as Paul ever came to proffering an apology, and she said, promptly and untruthfully, "No, of course not. I slept fine."

"Good. Um . . . I'd like for you to go over to the probate court when it opens. Sign us up on the hearing calendar, earliest date you can get."

She smiled with relief. "You're going to get a court order to change the will, then? You're not going to try to slip it by?"

"Right. You don't mess with the IRS. The hearing will not be a pleasant experience, but it'll turn out okay."

"You found the mistake?"

"Oh, yes. There's draft after draft that's perfect, and then, suddenly, in a draft from last April, it's wrong. *April.* Can you believe it? The curse of the Elkin will, lurking deep in the verbiage, waiting to spring."

"And could you tell if—"

"No. I don't know who made the mistake in the first place." He smiled at the wall a foot or so above her head. This attempt at good humor was costing him. "Forget about that, Meg, will you? In fact, you can enjoy the privilege of forgetting all about the Elkins for a while. I envy you."

With that the subject was closed between them. When she returned from the probate court, to tell him they had a date in early December, he only nodded. For the rest of that day, and all of the next, he did not mention the Elkins to her at all. By the day after that, the edge was coming off of Megan's expectancy. She knew that Paul was making occasional, soothing calls to Barbara Elkin, and having meetings with Arthur Lasch, the head of the trusts and estates department, but her own involvement seemed to have come to an end with her errand to the probate court. So the Elkin crisis subsided to a low buzz at the back of her head. Like most of the things she worried about, it was not going to live up to her fears.

This was how things seemed to Megan, as she went to lunch on Thursday afternoon.

There was a cafeteria on the ground floor of the building, where you could usually count on getting a quick meal if you arrived after the noon rush. But today the line was moving slowly. Megan had made her choice of soups when she became aware of someone looking at her. She turned and caught a glimpse of a tall young man, standing just beyond the railing that demarcated the serving area. It wasn't anybody she knew, and she slid her tray along. When she neared the end of the line, where it slowed as people waited for their drinks and got their money out, she saw the young man again, standing just beyond the cash register. He had on tinted glasses, so their eyes did not meet, but there was a faint smile on his face as if he were waiting for her. She busied herself over her purse. Megan's figure had caused her agonies when she was a teenager—she was too tall and lean, too broad in the shoulders, and she didn't have enough curves. But the fashion had changed and now hers was the sort of figure men liked to look at. She still had not gotten used to it.

She paid, picked up her tray, and set off for the far corner of the cafeteria without looking in the man's direction. She put her magazine on the table and began to eat and read, still without looking up. Nonetheless she was aware that the man had come over and was standing across the table from her.

She determined not to look at him. She was, she knew, one of those people who attracted beggars, crazies, and the troubled, in addition to guys on the make. Her forbearance must shine out from her.

He would not go away, though. She readied a few curt words in her mind, and raised her eyes.

He pointed his finger at her and said, "Megan Lofting, am I right?"

Megan could only stare, as umbrage gave way to apprehension that she had forgotten somebody she ought to know. It lasted only a moment: surely she couldn't know anyone who looked like this. He was in his mid-twenties, a few years younger than she, and he was coiffed and dressed at the height of a fashion that was quite exotic to her. His hair was cut to a military shortness at the sides and back, but with a sort of forties-movie-star wave at the top, and he was wearing a cara-mel-colored, double-breasted suit, the jacket open to reveal a lustrous pink T-shirt. She never saw people turned out like this in real life, but only on television or in New York. "I'm sorry," she said. "I don't—how do you know me?"

The man took this as an invitation to sit down. He placed his coffee cup on the table and settled himself comfortably. "We've never met, but I recognized you from the sound of your voice. You have such a pleasant way of speaking. Quite unmistakable."

It seemed unlikely enough, but she realized that she recognized his voice too. It was a distinctive voice, soft yet cadenced and articulated, the sort of voice that headwaiters and expensive hairdressers have. She said, "I've talked to you on the phone?"

The man nodded, leaning forward to pull the tails of his

coat straight. "Yes. Often. You're the one who has to talk to me when Paul won't return my calls."

"Oh," Megan said. "You're Brian Elkin."

He seemed to have a moment's shyness at being identified. His gaze at last left her face and wandered off to the far corners of the room. "You have it in one, as the English say."

"Did you come up to see Paul?"

"Well, I can't quite make up my mind about that. I fully intended to when I got on the train, but once I got here I wasn't so sure. I've been dawdling over this appalling coffee for more than an hour." He made it sound as if the quality of the coffee was somehow responsible for his indecision.

"Did you phone for an appointment?"

Brian wrinkled his nose. "Oh no."

"But he's not here. He's in a luncheon meeting at the Downtown Club. It could drag on for hours."

Brian did not sound disappointed. "Oh, I'm in no hurry. And I'm sure he isn't."

"Were you wanting to talk to him about your trust?"

His wandering gaze returned to her now, and he smiled.

"Oh no," he said. "You see, I know what's going on."

Megan dropped her eyes to her tray. She did not want to hear any more of this. She knew that she ought to get up and leave, right now. But it would be hard to do so gracefully when her meal was hardly touched.

"So how's friend Paul doing these days? A little nervous, maybe?"

"Not that I'm aware of," said Megan, keeping her eyes down. "Why do you think he should be nervous?"

Brian laughed. "Hey, that's a shrink's trick. Always answer a question with a question." But he was evidently enjoying himself, and he could not resist explaining. "Yesterday I got a call from a guy I know here in Stamford. A lawyer. He'd been over at the probate court, and he happened to see my name on the calendar. Elkin, that is. And he got curious and did some asking around in the clerk's office. Lawyers are such busybodies, aren't they? But this time I was glad to hear about it."

Megan pushed her tray aside. "I think you'd better talk to Paul about this. He'll be back later this afternoon."

Brian leaned forward. "You're here now, and I'm asking you. How come I wasn't informed about this?"

"You would have been. You would have received a notice in the mail. There's nothing secret about this. It's just routine."

"Oh, come on. I doubt very much that a will construction hearing—that is what they call it, right?—is ever routine. Why didn't Paul call me himself?"

"I suppose Paul felt that you weren't affected by the situation."

"But the problem is this phrase 'and issue,' isn't it? Well, 'issue' includes me."

He delved into a pocket of his bulky coat and took out a thick sheaf of photocopies—the will—which he dropped on the table. "You think my lawyer and I can't read? Once we knew Paul had screwed up, it wasn't too difficult to find out where he'd screwed up." He tapped his finger loudly on the will. "I know what this means. All Dad's children can get into the residuary trust. Little Harry, little Billy, little Barbi, and me."

He shoved the will across the table at her. Megan had resolved to say as little as possible, but Brian had such a gift for obnoxiousness that he managed to get a rise even from her. "It doesn't say that at all. It says that the money is left to Paul in trust. It's supposed to say that he can make payments only to Mrs. Elkin. Because of the mistake it reads that he could make payments to the children, too. But only if he wanted to."

In her irritation she had not phrased this in the neutral way the law preferred, and Brian took her up on it. "Only if he wanted to. And we know how Paul feels about me, don't we?"

"I have no idea how he—"

"Next you'll be telling me it would be folly for me to challenge the almighty Paul. I've heard that before." Brian drew himself upright. In his T-shirt and padded jacket, his neck looked long and frail, and his shorn hair made his face seem gaunt. But his voice, as it filled with indignation, grew plummier than ever. "I know there's no way to get around Paul. He keeps cropping up under a different hat. Counsel for the estate. Executor. Trustee of the residuary trust. Trustee of my trust. But what it comes down to is, he works for Barbara."

He paused dramatically, and Megan thought how strange

it sounded for him to say "Barbara." But what was a grown-up son to call his stepmother, except her first name? He must have called her Barbara from the beginning. He would have been in his teens when his father remarried; already too late to start calling this new woman Mother. She had a sudden glimpse into what lay behind Brian's posing and his troublesomeness, and it was an unwelcome glimpse. She said, "Look, Mr. Elkin. There's no point in telling me all this. I'm just a paralegal. My job is filling out forms and doing accounts. I don't make decisions. I don't even know about them."

He gazed at her steadily through his misty glasses. "You know about little things that you and I talk about on the phone. You know how I'm treated. Even if it's just an overdue credit-card bill, or a car loan, Paul makes it as difficult for me as he can. Well, now it's my turn to make things difficult for him."

He sat back now, smiling. "I have nothing to lose," he went on, airily, "I know that. I know what they're doing to me. They hide it all with trusts and powers of appointment and so on. But the simple truth is, I'm the first-born son, and they've swindled me out of my patrimony."

He picked up the will and pushed his chair back. Megan said hastily, "Mr. Elkin, please come upstairs. I'll call Paul out of his meeting and—"

"I don't care to talk to him right now. Tell him I'm in town, will you? Tell him I'm . . . taking legal advice, as the English say. That has the right ominous ring to it."

He swung round and walked away.

An hour later Megan was sitting in the big corner office of Arthur Lasch, telling Lasch and Paul the story of what had happened. She had telephoned the Downtown Club as soon as she returned to the office, gotten hold of Paul, and breathlessly explained. He heard her out in silence so complete that at times she lost the sense of there being anyone on the line. At the end he said simply that they would have to inform Lasch and that he was on his way back. Now he was standing at the window—which in this vast office seemed very far away—leaving her to face Lasch across his large desk.

Fortunately she had never felt daunted by him, even though he was the second most senior partner and the head of the

29

estates department. He was a small, plump, round-shouldered man, and his only notable features were heavy black spectacles and a furrowed brow. When Megan finished the story, he said, "Well, I think that . . . uh . . . then lapsed into silence. He was such an anxious, circumspect man that at times each sentence he uttered seemed to be a little hill that he had to get a running start to get over.

"I think that that was an unfortunate—unfortunate meeting, wasn't it? I'm not at all sure, Megan, that you should have talked to Mr. Elkin at all."

"Oh, come on, Arthur," Paul said. "The guy sat down at her table. What was she supposed to do, get up and leave? That wouldn't have done anything to improve his mood. Megan told him nothing, and he told us a lot. In fact, I think this lawyer he's got—or who's got him—is going to be pretty mad when he finds out how much Brian tipped their hand."

"Yes, what about this lawyer, Paul? It all sounds rather . . . uh, sounds rather dubious."

"I'm sure it is. Brian has an extensive acquaintance among lawyers, especially the more dubious kind. He's been involved in a lot of litigation. He's an entrepreneur of sorts. He starts businesses, and they fail, and the creditors come after him. He also has a way of cracking up cars while under the influence of various things."

"Yes. You certainly"—Lasch gave his wheezing chuckle— "you certainly get to know a lot of lawyers that way. So what do you think this fellow is trying to do for him?"

"They're bluffing. Brian's guy isn't really thinking of opposing me at the will construction hearing. He can't win, and even if he could, he knows that I could still prevent Brian from getting any money."

"Still, Paul, they could make things pretty damned unpleasant for you. I mean . . . they could come into court and say that there was no mistake. Try to defend the will. And there you'd be, the fellow who wrote the will, saying it was wrong. What a scene that would be."

Paul folded his arms and leaned back against the wall beside the window. "I'd rather have an unopposed hearing, obviously. They know that. They're planning to throw a scare into me. Then they'll offer me a deal. My guess is they'll ask

30

me to invade Brian's trust. He's not supposed to get the principal until he's thirty. I expect he'd like to get all of it now, and so would his lawyer."

"Is that," Lasch inquired, "is that all he wants? A payoff?"

"I think so."

Lasch hunched unhappily in his chair for a while. To her surprise, Paul asked, "What do you think, Megan?"

"Well, I don't know what his lawyer is planning, but what he said to me was that he wanted to make things difficult for you."

Lasch's eyebrows ascended briefly above his spectacle frames. "Does Brian have something against you, Paul?"

"Nothing personal. He just hates me in loco parentis."

"Oh, yes. He and his father did not get along, did they?" Paul said nothing, and after a long pause Lasch went on. "Well, obviously not. If they had, he would have taken a substantial inheritance at Mr. Elkin's death and we would not be . . . would not be having this problem now."

There was another pause, and then Lasch placed his hands flat on his neat, almost bare desktop, and said, "Paul, I think you ought to do . . . do whatever is necessary to placate Brian."

Paul shut his eyes for a moment—it was only a flicker of frustration—and then his face was expressionless again, and he spoke in the same brisk, neutral tone he had been using all along. "If we call his bluff he'll back down. He and his lawyer aren't going to oppose me at the hearing. They know they have nothing to gain."

"Paul. You've never . . . you've never gone to court on anything, have you?"

"Sure. Lots of times. When I was with Legal Aid—"

"Yes, yes. But I mean since you've been with this firm. In our field, you know, in our field we don't end up in court unless something's gone very wrong. Very wrong indeed. And once you get into a courtroom, anything can happen." He stared at his folded hands; his manner was even more abstracted than usual. "I've been involved in a couple of these things, these stepchild vs. stepparent wars. They can get nasty. You're dealing with emotions that run deep. The . . . the deepest emotions people have. Terribly strong emotions that . . ."

They waited, but this time Lasch did not get up the hill. He sat in silence, hunched over, and his brow rippled with worry. They could only wait until he looked up. "Give Brian the principal from the trust, if that will make him happy. He feels wronged. There's no telling what he might do. It's not worth it, Paul."

"It wouldn't make him happy. If he got it, most of it would go to lawyers and creditors. Then he'd be back to make more trouble." Paul came up to the desk now, but he did not sit down. "I'm sorry, Arthur, but at this point it's no concern of yours or mine whether Brian feels wronged. Hal Elkin's money was his to do with as he pleased. He wanted his wife and his younger children to get most of it. I'm his executor, and it's my job to see that his wishes are carried out."

Lasch looked profoundly unhappy. He put his hands in his lap, and slumped so low in his chair that he seemed about to disappear below the level of the desk. "I don't like the . . . the way that this is going, Paul. Don't like it at all. It started out as a simple mistake, and now it's threatening to turn into a fiasco."

"They're bluffing. All we have to do is sit tight and—"

"Yes, yes," Lasch interrupted querulously. "I know what you think. I . . . I also have reason to believe that you're not infallible, Paul. What I must do now is call Mrs. Elkin."

"Call Mrs. Elkin? Why?"

"To inform her of what's happening, and to make sure that you have her support."

"Arthur, there's no need to report Brian's wild talk to her. Let's at least wait till the lawyer contacts us before we get her all upset."

"No. I'm sorry, but I can't let you go out on a limb any farther. I have to talk to Mrs. Elkin."

"There's no reason for you to get involved at this stage. I'm the executor. It's my problem."

But Lasch wasn't paying attention to him anymore. He was staring balefully at the telephone. Paul turned away and left the office.

Megan got up to follow, and Lasch glanced up at her, as if he had forgotten she was there. He should have dismissed her as soon as she finished her account. It was unseemly for a paralegal to be present when partners were arguing. Megan almost wished that he had; she had been present at too many crises lately.

She caught up with Paul in the corridor. "Paul, what's going to happen?"

"It doesn't seem to be up to me to say." He went into his office, and shut the door behind him.

5

Megan spent the rest of the afternoon in her office, balancing an estate checking account. Like so much of her work, it was a mindless but meticulous task. She found that it absorbed and soothed her: it was the mental equivalent of pacing the floor. Her worries receded to the periphery of her mind. She even lost track of time.

"Megan?"

She jumped so that her pencil scratched a long line through a column of figures. Arthur Lasch's small, stooped figure stood in her doorway. "Can I come in for a moment?"

"Oh, of course."

There was an extra chair in the room, but since Megan seldom had visitors it stood by the desk, serving as shelf-space. She quickly took the books and papers off of it, but Lasch did not seem to want to sit down. He slumped against the wall, shoved his hands deep into his pockets, and frowned at the top of her desk. As usual, he was having a hard time getting going.

Megan asked, "Did you speak to Mrs. Elkin?"

"Yes. I spoke to her for quite some time. She was very difficult, very upset. There was all sorts of . . . all sorts of wild talk. I'm afraid that this is only the beginning. It's going to be a drawn-out and unpleasant business. Word will get around the firm soon enough. And that will be especially hard on you. People are going to be leery of you. They won't want to give you work. So I think it's best for you and us if you leave now."

"Leave?" she echoed, not understanding.

"I'm sorry, Megan, but I have to ask you to leave the firm."

In that first moment she was too surprised to grasp what was happening to her. She had sometimes imagined being fired, but not by Arthur Lasch, not in this gentle, fumbling manner. In her astonishment she blurted, "Have you talked to Paul about this?"

Lasch did not reply. He was staring fixedly down at her desk, as if there were a prepared text there from which he could not depart. "You really won't want to be here, once people start losing confidence in you. A probate paralegal has to be, has to be meticulous. Has to be a bit of a plodder. Someone like you gets bored with the work, starts to make mistakes. Really, you're too bright for the job."

"It's the only job I have!" Megan burst out. Her voice was raw and angry, and hearing it fed her anger. "My God. You act like you're doing me a favor, firing me. What are these mistakes you're talking about? What mistakes have I made? I had to talk to Brian Elkin. You heard Paul say that. I couldn't avoid it."

"Oh, it's not that." Lasch sighed and went on, "All right. I suppose you have a right to know. It's her. Mrs. Elkin. I kept trying to get her to be reasonable, to give us a line on how she wants Brian dealt with. But she was too upset. She kept demanding to know how we could let this happen in the first place. How we could let you work on her estate, how we could place a person like you in a position of trust."

"A person like me? What does she mean, a person like me?"

Lasch looked at her now, for the first time.

"Megan, you told her yourself that it was your fault."

It was true. She had done that. She'd forgotten. But she

remembered now, how she had stumbled through her apology and her long explanation as Barbara Elkin stared at her, uncomprehending and fearful. "Oh no," she mumbled. "No . . . Paul said it wasn't my fault. He said it could have been anybody . . . have you talked to Paul about this?"

Arthur Lasch stared blankly at her for a moment. "Why, yes. Of course I have."

A surge of anguish rose up from deep inside her and blocked her throat. Her eyes prickled with hot tears. Oh no, she said to herself, I'm not going to cry. She put her hands up to her cheeks. There were no tears. She began to take deep breaths, and kept at it until she could do so without shuddering. In a moment she would be able to talk again.

Lasch took no notice of her struggle. His gaze had returned to the desktop, and he was speaking in that hesitant, back-and-forth way of his. It was something about the disposition of her files. He was back to pretending that this was not a terrible thing that was being done to her.

She realized suddenly that there was no reason why she had to go on sitting here and listening to him. She got up and came around the desk. Lasch broke off what he was saying and shrank back against the wall as she passed.

Paul was talking on the telephone. When she came in, he said, "I'll call you back, okay?" and put the receiver down. Then he rose and walked behind her to close the office door.

She waited until he was sitting down again. Then she said: "You're letting them do this to me."

He leaned back and folded his hands behind his neck, so that his elbows jutted out on either side of his unyielding face. "It was all over by the time I heard about it. Lasch was the one who had to call her up. Had to get her scared and mad, and this is the result. There was nothing I could do."

"Nothing?"

"You set yourself up for this, Megan. You don't apologize to clients. Will you just grow up and figure that out? Kids can apologize. They fess up and get sent to bed without supper and then everything's fine. Only that doesn't work any more when you're a grown-up. Grown-ups don't apologize. They cover their ass. I don't know where you got this crazy idea that I could protect you."

"I suppose it's because I would have stood up for you."

The rigid nonchalance of his pose cracked. He leaned forward and turned his face away from her. "I don't know what that's supposed to mean. In this situation what could I have said to Lasch without letting him know that—?" The door was closed, but he dropped his voice to a whisper anyway. "Don't you understand, I couldn't say anything because of our relationship?"

"No, I don't. Our relationship is why I would have said something."

The phone began to ring. Paul glanced at it and left it alone. "Look, Meg. Why don't you go home now? I'll get back as soon as I can. Then we'll talk."

Megan did not answer. She was beginning to feel weak now. All that had happened was catching up to her. The shock and anger would not bear her up for much longer. But Paul had said "home" and that had reminded her of one last thing to be done. She reached into her jacket pocket for her key ring. She began to detach the key to Paul's apartment. Her fingers were stiff and trembling, and she had to fumble at it for a long time. Paul said, "What is this, some kind of grand gesture?"

She did not feel like replying. At last she worked the key off and laid it on his desk. It make a small, definite click against the wood. She turned away and went out. Behind her Paul was saying something about calling her.

The corridor was full of noise and people. She didn't look at anyone; she was no longer one of them. It seemed to take a long time to reach the heavy double doors and get through them to the hush and dimness of the lobby. She heard the receptionist say, "You leaving for the day, Meg?" Then she was through the last set of doors and out.

6

The building Megan lived in was a noisy one, with thin walls and an echoing concrete stairwell. She had grown used to the noise and paid no attention to it. So the knocking had probably been going on for a while before she became aware of it.

She did nothing about it, and presently it ceased. She heard the footfalls fading down the stairs. At least Paul wasn't so persistent anymore. She wondered, though, why he had come back at all.

She raised her head from the tabletop upon which she had been resting it and peered out the window. The sun was making a pretty golden mist of the dust on her west window. It was evening, Sunday evening. Three days since she had been fired. Seventy-two hours, give or take one. Perhaps Paul had come back because he thought that by now, surely, she would have come to her senses.

"When you come to your senses—" They were the last words she had heard as she took the phone from her ear and hung it up. And she had heard them again, later, shouted through her door which she would not open. Paul seemed to set great store by the phrase. He seemed to think that her anger would die down, and her hurt heal, with the passage of a certain amount of time. He had nothing else to offer, for all the words he said—no explanation, no apology. But then Paul never did apologize.

This time he had given up without saying anything at all. She was grateful for that. She was also grateful that he did not have a key. There had been no reason to give him one, for they had never spent any time here. Now she was beginning to get used to the place again.

A sudden noise made her jump. She swung around in her chair. Her caller had come around the building and up the back steps to knock at her kitchen door—and it was not Paul. She could see only a blurred figure through the frosted glass, but it was someone shorter and slighter than Paul.

Megan struggled to her feet. Tonight of all nights. She ought to ask for a minute, and go tidy her face and clothes. At least hide the bottle. But none of that seemed terribly important. She took two unsteady steps to the door and opened it.

Brian Elkin stood there, with one hand upraised. He lowered it and smiled. "I knew it. I knew you were home."

"What are you doing here?"

"I heard what happened to you. That you'd been sacked, I mean." He was not wearing his tinted glasses now. He had dark, sunken eyes, beneath heavy brows. "I realize it's partly my fault."

"Yes. It is." Megan closed her eyes and rubbed her brow. That had not been a gracious thing to say, but at the moment no reason for being gracious to Brian Elkin occurred to her. Her other hand was still on the door. She began to swing it closed. "Go away, will you?"

Brian put up a hand to block the door. "Don't you even want to know how it turned out? *L'affaire* Elkin, I mean. Because it's all over now."

"It was all over for me three days ago. I don't want to hear."

Brian would not take his hand away. He said, "Have you been drinking?"

"Just—just leave, will you?"

"I was only going to ask for one myself." He gave a rueful shrug. "Come on. You and I are the two big losers here. Why don't we have a drink together?"

It was an artful suggestion; the whiskey in her veins seemed to long for company even if she did not. She let him in, and turned away to her seat at the table.

Brian took the chair beside her. He had gotten himself a big tumbler, and he filled it halfway, and topped up her own drink. "You haven't been drinking the whole time?"

She might have repelled sympathy if he had pressed it on her, but the question was so neutral that she answered it. "No. Just tonight. I don't know what I did that first night exactly."

"The shock must have been pretty bad."

"No. The shock was the good part. It was after it wore off that I got to thinking. Then things were really grim. But tonight's special. Tonight I'm drinking myself to sleep."

"You started early."

"Yes. I did. Tomorrow I have to pull myself together. It's Monday and I have to start looking for a job."

"I see." Brian took a long swallow. It might have been the whiskey playing tricks on her, but Megan felt that for a moment a genuine emotion registered on his elegant features. "I feel rotten about this. I really do. You were always so nice to me when we talked on the phone. I had no idea that—"

Megan interrupted, "You were going to tell me what happened."

"Oh. Right." The usual archness came back into his voice. "Your sacrifice was not in vain, if that makes you feel any better. The wrath of Barbara was propitiated. She put herself entirely in Paul's hands. And he proved worthy. He's scared the living shit out of my lawyer." Brian had settled into one of his poses now, legs crossed, left hand dangling off the knee. His other hand held the glass. She noticed that it was almost empty already. "The deed was done today, in fact. Paul invited my guy to brunch at the country club, then took him back to the office and showed him the evidence he's planning to produce at the hearing. Then he dropped a few veiled threats. See, my lawyer is not a pinstriper who pals around with judges, like Paul. He got scared and dropped me flat."

Brian leaned forward to pick up the bottle. As he poured, he glanced sideways at Megan. "So the way is clear to the hearing. You're going to come in handy then, too. Now that you're gone they can blame it all on you. Paul can say, 'Look at this gorgeous estate plan I drew up Judge, and then some incompetent paralegal had to screw it up.' The judge will say, 'Well, I hope you fired the dumb twat.' Or however you say that in court. And Paul will tell him, 'Hey, don't worry, Judge. She's history.' "

Megan shut her eyes tight. When she opened them, Brian was still watching her face. So, this was why he had come here: to try to make her angry. In some perverse way that would soothe his own hurt feelings. She said bluntly, "You were stupid to take Paul on."

"Oh, I know that. You think I don't know that? My lawyer—my ex-lawyer—told me all about how badly I'd handled it."

"He wouldn't have done any better. You were both counting on Paul being shaken because he'd made a mistake. Most people would be. But Paul's not like that."

Brian shrugged. "I guess you would know."

"Yes, I would. I used to be his girlfriend."

Brian drew his breath in sharply. "Oh my God, I had no idea. You can't lay that on me. That's too much."

"I don't mean to lay anything on you." Megan was not sure why she had told him, except that she had kept Paul's secret for so long, and the chance to give it away was irresistible. She took another drink. The whiskey tasted harsh and inimical, as it had on her first few swallows. When she moved her head, small fissures of pain opened in it, like seams tearing. It was a foretaste of what was coming tomorrow morning. Monday.

"You'll have to leave now. I'm going to bed. You can take the bottle if you want. In fact, I'd be glad if you'd take the bottle."

But Brian's face had turned grave, and he was not to be diverted from what he had to say. "I felt so charged up when I started this thing. I thought, finally, finally, I'm doing something. Now it's over, and the only result is that I got you fired, and I'm worse off than I was before. This kind of thing is always happening to me."

She held her dizzy head in both hands. She could not go to bed quite yet. "Brian, let's get one thing straight. This is not happening to you. You're going to be okay. You'll keep getting those quarterly checks from your trust. I don't think Paul is even mad at you."

"No, of course he's not. Why should he be mad at me? He

gets so much enjoyment out of my legal troubles. Barbara's probably not mad either. No—she is, but she'll forgive me. Barbara loves forgiving me. It's a holiday thing with her. Last June she forgave me on her birthday. Even invited me up. I shouldn't have come, but it was hot in the city. Tripped over her brats on the front steps, and there she was sunning on the veranda. She gets up, sagging out of her bikini, and comes and gives me a big wet sloppy kiss and tells me I can still be one of the family if I'll be good and stop talking about money all the time. She'll say the same again. Who can be mad at me? I'm only dangerous to myself. I'm my own worst enemy. Nobody else is even in the running."

His voice broke slightly on the last word, and he lapsed into silence. He sat slumped back, arms outflung along the arms of the chair, his chin sunk to his breast. It was a pose vaguely reminiscent of the Lincoln Memorial. His acute self-consciousness made her self-conscious too: she delved into her heart, and found not a trace of pity for him there. Perhaps it was because this measured self-denunciation of his had been worn smooth by too many repetitions to psychiatrists and friends and lovers. Perhaps it was the pain in her head. Megan hoped not. She hoped it was simply that she had grown a little tougher than she used to be.

"Listen, Brian," she said. "I have to get some sleep, for tomorrow. If I don't have a paycheck by the first of the month, I won't be able to pay the rent. I don't want to hear about your problems anymore. They're too complicated for someone like me." She hesitated; she was about to say "Please leave." But she had tried that before, without success. So she said, "Get out."

Brian rose slowly from his chair. He had that awful expression on his face again, that injured yet gratified smile. "It's not me you're mad at, you know," he said. "I just happen to have the decency to be here. It's them you're mad at, only they're not here."

She ought to let him have the last line, if that would get him out the door. But she heard herself replying, "I don't have time to waste being mad. I'm going to put this behind me and get on with my life."

"Put it behind you? No. It's inside you. It's eating away at you. You'll find out."

41

This time she did not respond, and Brian was content to leave her. The moment the door closed behind him, she staggered into the bedroom. She lay down without undressing, and in another moment she was asleep.

PART II

1

"Grand Central. Last stop. All change. Grand Central."

The voice muttering over the intercom was premature. The train was still crawling along, more and more slowly, as if it had lost its way in the underground labyrinth. Passengers were growing impatient. The group of teenagers across the aisle from Megan unhooked their Walkmans and got up, to stand swaying and chatting at the doors. The ladies on their way to luncheons and shopping expeditions began packing up their bulky handbags and squirming into their coats. Megan stayed put. She was in no hurry.

The train jolted to a halt and the doors opened. Megan got up and put on her overcoat and gloves. She took the backpack from the seat beside her and wrestled into the shoulder straps. She clamped the tennis racket under her arm and picked up the two suitcases, making sure that the heavier one was in her right hand. Then she went out into the warm, musty gloom of the platform. People from the cars further back were rushing past her on both sides. She supposed that she must be a sight, trundling along under her ill-assorted burdens. But then she remembered the conductor's saying, "All change," and felt better. For all these people knew, New York might not be her final destination. Perhaps she was going to board a gleaming Amtrak special, bound for someplace far to the west or south, where she would be needing a camping rig and a tennis racket. It was a nice fantasy.

She went through the gate into the vast, echoing concourse of the station. Peering over the heads of the hurrying crowds, she spotted the sign that said IRT, and headed for it. She passed a bakery, and went down a gallery lined with pizza joints and other snack bars. She made her way through the crowds, and gradually the aromas of bread, mustard, and oregano gave way to the smell of urine. She came to the arched portal marked SUBWAY, and the worn steps leading down. She put off breathing for a moment to consider, and thought better of it. Turning, she walked on toward the street, to look for a cab. This was not in the plan. She had not intended to spend money on a cab. But now that seemed foolish: if the day wasn't a success, small economies weren't going to help.

The bags were heavier than she had thought. Her shoulders were beginning to sag, her knees to give. Soon she was walking like a plover on a beach, in a flat, swift scurry. But this was the last dim hallway. Ahead, through the row of glass doors, she could see the traffic passing on Lexington Avenue.

Here, as always, were the ragged men approaching to mutter and hold out their hands, and the bundles of greasy clothes against the wall, with only a knobby, weathered face showing, or a swollen ankle, the skin pink and splotched like the endpapers of expensive books. In the old days when she used to come down to the city with Paul, she used to think of these hallways as a gauntlet to be run. She would grip his arm, avert her eyes, and hurry along with high heels clicking, trying to pay attention to what he was saying about the restaurant or the play. She wondered why she couldn't be suavely oblivious to these wretched people, the way he was. But now, no longer having his example to emulate, she paused and set down her case when a figure stepped in her way, mumbling about spare change. If she was taking a cab, she could spare a quarter.

She felt good as she walked on, felt reckless and enterprising. Perhaps she would do very well, today. Perhaps she wouldn't have to keep anxious count of her pocket change anymore. She bumped her way through the doors, dropped the suitcases at the curb, and raised her arm for a taxi.

Fifteen minutes later she was standing before a small shopfront. Its window display consisted of a large, dreary oil painting in an ornate frame, a faded gown that someone had worn to a ball in the thirties, and a tea service in an unattractive pattern, the cups turned this way and that to hide the chips. SECOND CHANCE THRIFT, said the sign above the window.

Megan turned to look up the block and then across the street. She saw the signs of other thrifts. So what she had heard was correct: secondhand stores were clustered all along upper Third Avenue, and she had her choice of which to go into. But this was not a moment for hesitation. The Second Chance Thrift would do.

She went in and staggered down the narrow aisle to the counter at the back. A young man got up and came over to her, sliding his hands into his pants pockets. He raised his eyebrows but said nothing.

"Good morning. I have some things to sell."

"Okay. Let's see."

She had expected to be invited to a back office, but apparently it wasn't done that way. She shrugged out of the backpack and laid it on the counter, then heaved the suitcases up beside it and opened them.

The man leaned forward, still with his hands in his pockets. "You're selling all this?"

"Yes."

"Okay." He chose to examine the backpack first. He was bearded and fit-looking; perhaps he was an outdoorsman himself. After glancing in the compartments and poking the taut cocoon of the sleeping bag he said, "We don't get much call for camping equipment this time of year, but it's a pretty nice rig."

Megan bestirred herself to a little salesmanship. "It's almost new. Bought this summer and only used once."

"Oh yeah? Where'd you go?"

"Vermont."

"No kidding? I used to go up there a lot. What trail were you on?"

Megan hesitated. It didn't seem right for him to ask these questions. A man in a secondhand shop ought to show the same professional indifference toward your possessions that a doctor showed toward your body. "Franconia Park," she murmured. "Around in there." And then she thought she had better turn away.

She blinked and swallowed hard, and felt all right again. Behind her, the man was saying, "Got some nice sailing gear here. Wrong season again, though." So now he was pawing through the brightly striped jerseys and the yellow squall suit. She did not reply, for in a moment he would get to the hand-knit sweaters and tweed knickers, the suede jacket and skiing boots. He would get to the right season. There were plenty of Paul's gifts to choose from.

Paul liked to be well-equipped when he went back to nature, and it had cost him a small fortune to buy similar accoutrements for her. The Friday-night rush to get away had always begun with a stop at the safari boutiques of the mall. Paul relaxed once he was on the mountain or in the woods, but until he got there he was brusque and edgy. She had had the feeling that if she tried to decline any of his presents, he would leave her behind. So she had accepted them.

It had not occurred to her to sell them until one evening earlier this week. Then she had opened the back door to take the garbage out, and had found a pair of big cardboard boxes on her doorstep. They were damp from the rains, but the contents were undamaged: her books, her clothes and toiletries—everything she had left at Paul's apartment, right down to a half-empty bottle of shampoo. To collect all these things must have involved a major sacrifice of time for such a busy and untidy man. She wondered if it was a discreet precaution, in preparation for a new girlfriend, or if he just wanted to remove every trace of her from his home.

She could not return the favor. There was nothing of his in her apartment. It was then that she remembered the things that he had given her. She could box them up and leave them on his doorstep and slip away, just as he had done. But what was the point of returning them? He had his own tennis racket and backpack, and he would have no use for women's clothes unless there really was another girlfriend who was as poorly equipped as she had been. No, she needed them more than he did. They were assets to be liquidated, and she had to have some cash.

She had put off facing the things until late last night. Then they had come down from the shelves and out of the closets, and, as she had feared, there were memories wrapped up in them like sweet fragrances, and the memories had burst upon her. There were the expected ones, of lovely vistas and shared silences, and lovemaking in odd places, but there was one image she had not expected at all: Paul listening to her. She was a country girl, while he was a suburbanite who studied trail guides, and she knew more about the natural world than he. He used to question her, and listen to her, as he seldom did in their day-to-day lives. She could see his grave, attentive face, and the memory was as clear, as unreal, as a scene in a movie.

Megan had given in to her tears thinking of him. Then she packed the presents up and went to bed, resolved to sell them all tomorrow. Perhaps when they were gone, Paul would become smaller and dimmer in her mind.

The salesman called for her attention. He rapped each item, and briskly named a price. It seemed that he was going to take all of Paul's gifts, even the unseasonal ones, so she would be left with only her own belongings to take to the next shop.

When the check was in her hand, she thought that the total was rather less than she had hoped for, considering all he had taken. But at least her suitcases were lighter. She picked them up and set off up the street to the next thrift.

She did not do as well there. She was only able to get rid of a couple of pairs of shoes and a clock-radio. In the third place there was a lugubrious old man, who shook his head and groaned as he pawed through her summer dresses and kitchen odds-and-ends, and despairingly told her that this sort of merchandise did not move. Her fourth stop was brief: a hard-eyed woman with great encrustations of earrings looked her up and down and told her they weren't buying today, and made it sound as if Megan was a fool not to know that.

Megan was not insulted. That was the good thing about New York: she wasn't so sensitive here. She didn't take things personally. There were so many people jostling one another that it seemed absurd to take offense. The rudeness, along with the noise and dirt and rush, glazed over one's sensibilities. Nothing in New York seemed quite real; it didn't seem to be happening to her. So she kept on going up Third Avenue, until the thrift shops petered out, and then crossed the street and started down the other side. She had gotten rid of a few more things, including the suitcases themselves. She was now carrying the remainder of her belongings in plastic shopping bags.

She had been at it for almost two hours when she came to a shop she couldn't bring herself to go in. She looked through its big windows, and saw people rummaging through troughs of junk under the eyes of prowling clerks, and decided to skip the place. She walked on, and two doors down she came to the Raymond Gallery.

It was the window display that caught her attention. Instead of the forlorn clutter she was used to seeing, this window was composed and lit like a stage set. It was an end table flanked by chairs. The fabric of the seat coverings shone like polished metal, and the tabletop had a deep, even luster like a Thoroughbred's coat. There was a display of silver knickknacks resting on it, and a card in a silver frame, lettered like a wedding invitation: "We are pleased to accept, on a sale or consignment basis, gold, silver, and other objects of value."

Megan's hand slipped into her pocket and touched the hard round shape of the watch. It was an antique, a silver watch of the sort that Gibson girls used to wear pinned to the shoulders of their blouses. Paul had given it to her on her birthday.

She had kept it back because she wasn't at all sure she had the right to sell it. Instead she ought to return it to Paul. It was all right to sell the other things that he had pressed upon her. But the watch was a true gift, one he had given careful thought to. And it was probably worth a lot of money.

Suddenly, right on the crowded pavement, she laughed—a real laugh that sent a jet of vapor into the cold air. It was one of those moments, occurring more and more frequently of late, when she would step back and regard herself with amazement. Was she really planning to pass up the Raymond Gallery's invitation, and continue down the street, trying to sell her paltry belongings for a few dollars, when she had this watch in her pocket? That was the way scrupulous, doomed heroines behaved in Victorian novels. It was what Tess of the d'Urbervilles or Lily Bart would do. But not she. Her hand closed around the watch, and she stepped up to the door of the Raymond Gallery and rang its bell.

The door buzzed open, and she walked down a narrow aisle lined with pieces of furniture, chiffoniers and highboys and a long dining table. The woodwork glowed in the soft light from the row of crystal chandeliers above her. Otherwise the shop was pleasantly dark and smelled faintly of polish. It wasn't a secondhand store at all, but an antique shop.

She went to the counter and stated her business, and the salesgirl went to fetch the owner. A moment later a man emerged from the back of the shop. He grinned at her, as if spotting a friend across a crowded room, and strode over.

"Hi, I'm Mr. Raymond. What can I do for you?"

Megan nearly blinked to look at him: in the gloom of the shop he was effulgent. He had a ruddy face, and glossy light brown hair, and he was wearing a double-breasted blazer with bright buttons and a crimson handkerchief in the pocket. Megan mustered up a smile that seemed feeble before Mr. Raymond's, and wordlessly laid the watch on the counter.

"What a beautiful thing!" he exclaimed, with an unguardedness that was a novelty for her today. "Excuse me while I take a closer look."

He took the watch over to the side and examined it with the tools of his trade, humming to himself all the while. Next he opened a big book and ran his finger down a column of figures. Then he returned and laid the watch on the counter between them. Megan braced herself to hear that it wasn't in top condition or wasn't the sort of thing that moved, or any of the other derogatory comments that always preceded an offer.

Mr. Raymond said only, "Five and a quarter."

"You mean, five hundred and twenty-five dollars?"

"Right."

She repeated the figure to herself. It was twice what she had raised on all the other things put together. By itself, it put her over her most optimistic goal for the day. She felt a pleasant twinge, to see her newfound lack of scruples so promptly rewarded.

Mr. Raymond misread her silence. He said, "That's a good price. You want to get some more bids that's fine with me. My offer stands."

"Oh, that's all right. I accept. Thank you."

Mr. Raymond was smiling, and she realized that she was positively beaming at him. The watch disappeared promptly under the counter, and he said, "Come on in back and we'll take care of the formalities." The dark eyes in his florid face were acute. "If you don't mind my saying so, you look like you wouldn't mind taking the load off your feet."

She realized that she had not sat down since she'd gotten out of the cab. Nodding gratefully, she stooped to pick up her bags.

"I'll take those," said Mr. Raymond gallantly. He led the way down a narrow and surprisingly long corridor—the shop, like so many places in New York, had unexpected depths—to his office. The armchair in front of his desk was deep and comfortable, and Megan found it so pleasurable to sit down that for a moment she closed her eyes.

"Coffee?" he called out, from somewhere behind her.

"Oh, yes. Thank you."

He returned with it in a moment—two china cups and saucers, on a silver tray, with matching creamer and sugar bowl. He set the tray down on the desk between them. It was a small, ornate desk, covered in red leather and festooned with brass.

"Thank you, Mr. Raymond," she said, beguiled by this sudden effusion of elegance and hospitality.

"Call me Ray," he replied, as if she were going to have many occasions for doing so, as if this were the beginning of a long acquaintance. "Actually, my name's Raymond Klausner,

52

but the "Klausner Gallery" didn't have quite the right ring to it, you know? And you are?"

"Oh. Sorry. I'm Megan Lofting."

"Megan. Pretty name."

"Is it? I don't know, I suppose it's a sweet name for a little girl. But you ought to be allowed to change it when you get to be fourteen."

Ray Klausner stopped smiling and his brows drew together in puzzlement. He turned a little away from her, to get a receipt pad and checkbook out of the drawer. She realized that it had been an odd thing to say to a stranger, but she had grown unused to conversation. These last few weeks she'd had only herself to talk to, and her tone was often harsh.

He took her name and address down on the receipt. "One watch, five twenty-five. Unless you've got something else in there you'd care to show me?" He pointed his gold pen at the plastic bags, which were slumped against the side of the desk.

"No. That's just some old clothes and things. You wouldn't be interested."

He raised his eyebrows.

"I've been going to the shops along here, trying to sell things."

"Oh, geez. Those guys." He gave the New Yorker's grimace and dismissive wave. "I wish you'd come here first. I could've given you some tips at least. Warned you off the worst of them. Not that any of them are much good. They make you feel lousy, and they pay you shit. Pardon my language."

She took a sip of coffee. "It doesn't matter. I'm finished now."

"Still, working the thrifts—that's a terrible thing to have to do. You sure there's nothing in here I could help you with?"

"No, really. I—"

But he had already opened one of the bags and was peering into it. "Books? You've been lugging books around? I could have told you you wouldn't get anything for them."

"Just the one," Megan said. "It's a foreign edition. I thought it might be worth something."

Now that she had said that, of course, he had to take the

53

volume out and open it. His eyes fell on the plate at the front. He grinned. "Third form French Prize. So you won this in high school. Pardon me. Prep school." He ran his finger over the plate where the name of the school was engraved, and then looked up at her, with the same sort of fond, appraising gaze he had earlier given to the watch. "I've heard of this place, of course. You know, my clients talking about how they'd kill to get their kids in. So you actually went there?"

She shrugged. "I only got to go because my father taught there."

This set off more ripples in his active brow. "Hey, don't run yourself down like that. You want me to think you weren't smart enough to get in without pull? But you must've been plenty smart to win this prize."

"I only meant that I couldn't have gone if my fees hadn't been waived."

"Oh, sure. Place like this must cost a bundle." He was still holding the book open, looking at the plate. "You must have gotten to know some real special people. Been invited to some terrific places."

"Well, my classmates would invite me for visits sometimes, if that's what you mean."

"Sure. Ski lodges. Beach houses. Pieds à terre here in town. How come you're looking at me funny like that? I guess my French isn't up to your standard, huh?"

She had not realized that she was letting her amusement show. She said hastily, "No, it's not that. It's just that I don't remember visiting my friends' houses as being all that much fun."

"It wasn't fun?"

"It was a lot of work, really."

"Work?"

"When you can't repay people—when you don't have a ski lodge or a beach house to invite them to, you feel you ought to make yourself useful. You keep an eye on the appetizer tray, in case it needs passing. You check on everybody's glass, to see who needs a refill. That's tricky because all the time you're listening so hard to people. Trying to take an interest in whatever they're saying, to laugh when they want you to. It's hard work pleasing people. It wears you out." Megan's heart had

54

started to beat fast, and her limbs were tense. She put the cup and saucer on the desk, setting them down so hard that they clattered. "Sorry," she said. "I don't mean to make it sound like such an ordeal. I didn't mind then. But I don't like thinking about it now."

Ray Klausner was watching her intently. That made her nervousness even sharper, and she said, "I'd like that check, please."

"Sure. Whatever you say." He closed the book between his palms and put it away, then slid the bags towards her. In silence he filled out the check. He stood up to hand it over, and their eyes met.

"Here you go. Good luck. I hope this gives you some help with your problems."

She looked away. "I don't have any problems. There were some old things I wanted to get rid of."

"Whatever you say. But you been working the thrifts all day, you just sold me that beautiful watch, must have been in your family for generations. Seems to me you got problems, Megan."

"It hasn't been in the family for generations. It means nothing to me. I'm glad to get rid of it. I—" Suddenly her throat closed up. She braced herself and hunched over, to hide her face from the man. When she was able to look up, though, he wasn't there. He had made a tactful retreat to the other side of the room. A moment later he returned with the coffeepot, and refilled her cup.

"I don't want any more."

"That's okay. Just leave it."

He went back to his own side of the desk and sat down. He wrote another check and handed it to her, and only then did she realize she had crumpled the first one in her fist. She put the wadded ball on the desk. "Sorry."

"No problem." He picked up his coffee and leaned back in his chair. "Maybe you want to talk."

"I think I've talked too much already."

"I don't think so. I mean, we're strangers. You don't have to worry what you tell me. And once you talk about your problems you get them out of your head. They're not so big any more. Not so special." He took a sip of coffee, watching her over the brim of the cup. "So what happened? You lose your job?"

Megan gave a long sigh. It seemed to her that her very next breath came more deeply, more easily. So maybe what he said was true. "I guess it isn't very special. How did you know?"

"Well, looking at you I wouldn't figure you for a drug habit or for blowing it all at the track, so what else is left?" He grinned and went on, "Now you're collecting unemployment, having a tough time making ends meet?"

"No, I've got another job."

"Good for you. Same line of work?"

"Not really. I'm a clerk-typist in a company that makes mailbox doors for apartment buildings."

"Uh-huh. So that's a stopgap, sort of, till you get something else in your line?"

"I don't know."

"What did you do, anyway?"

"I was a probate paralegal." At his blank look, she explained. "I was with a law firm, working on wills and trusts."

"That's interesting. That sounds very interesting."

"It wasn't really. It's very dry work."

"But better than what you got now. You don't want to go back to it?"

"Not especially."

"Cause of what happened to your old job? They fire you?" He spread his hands. "Hey, you can tell me. I used to get fired all the time. All the time. Finally had to make myself the boss."

"Yes," Megan replied. "They fired me."

Again, she felt better as soon as the words were out. When she had been looking for work, she had been put to so much finessing and fabrication over the question that it was exhilarating to speak the truth. She went on without waiting to be prompted. "There was a mistake in a rich man's will. I took the blame for it, even though it wasn't my fault. And when his widow got upset and wanted me fired, he—they—they went ahead and did it for her."

"Fuckers," said Ray Klausner. He did not beg pardon for his language this time. His face even seemed to have turned a deeper shade of red.

Megan shrugged. "If you go around trying to make yourself useful to people, they'll use you. There's no point in blaming them for it. You have only yourself to blame."

"But how are you getting along? You can't be making ends meet with this typing job. I mean, if you could you wouldn't be here."

"I've cut back where I can, but there are some things—I'm still paying off my college loan. I graduated eight years ago, and I'm still paying a hundred a month. And my rent is high, and I can't find a cheaper place—"

"Sure. Only way you can live in Stamford is if you've got a plush job at one of those big corporations they got up there. What can you do? This is New York metro. The fast track. It's no place to be if you're just trying to get by. How come you decided to stick it out here?"

"I don't know. I couldn't think of anywhere else to go."

"Your dad—the teacher—he's no longer living?"

"Both my parents are dead."

"Oh, I'm sorry. No sisters or brothers?"

"I have a sister. Back home in New Hampshire."

"Uh-huh. What'd she say when you told her?"

"I haven't told her. Well, not all of it."

Ray Klausner rolled his eyes. "You Wasps kill me. When I was out of work I used to go freeload off every relative I had. Now, they come freeload off me. Why haven't you told her? Afraid she wouldn't help?"

"Oh no. Gail's very nice. She couldn't give me money— she's got house payments, and a little boy, and she's divorced. But she'd invite me to come live with her."

"So?"

"I guess what I'm afraid of is that I'd go."

Ray Klausner waited.

"I know what would happen. It would be hard for me to get a job up there—any kind of job. So I'd be stuck around the house. So I'd help out."

"Sure. Cook. Clean. Baby-sit. Make yourself useful, in other words."

She looked up sharply at him. "Yes. I'd make myself useful. And I'm sort of fed up with that."

Ray nodded. He slid his French cuff back from his large

57

gold watch. "It's almost two. Want to grab a bite to eat? There's an okay place around the corner."

Megan was taken by surprise. She replied automatically, "Thank you, but I have to be going."

"Do you really?" Ray Klausner asked.

She smiled, for in truth she had no appointments until work on Monday morning. "No, not really."

Ray was on his feet, adjusting his tie, smoothing his lapels. "Come on. It's on me."

"All right," she said. "Thanks."

2

The restaurant he took her to was a fashionable place. Following the headwaiter, they slipped sideways between crowded rows of tables where people were eating with their elbows clamped to their sides, and bending over the table to try to catch a word their companions were saying. But it was to a secluded booth at the back that the headwaiter led them: obviously Mr. Raymond was known here.

The ordering involved a series of waiters, and took a long time. Ray Klausner, like so many men who were in the business of style, took his pleasures seriously. He wanted to know all about spices and cooking methods, and required an inventory of the wine cellar. In all the fuss, Megan's order of the cheapest salad on the menu sank without trace, and she ended up joining him for the special and a bottle of wine.

The food was excellent, and Ray, giving her the inside story on chefs and galleries, was lively company. But Megan took care to make her first glass of wine last through the meal. There was something odd about all this. For her, of course, simply to take a meal in company was an event, but beyond that there was something peculiar in his working so hard to draw her out, and spending so much time and money to impress her. It couldn't be for the usual reason. Megan knew that, dressed as she was today, she was quite safe from a man who valued appearances as highly as Raymond Klausner did. He was watching her so attentively that his eyes even followed the motion of her fork to her mouth, but it was the sort of gaze that made her skin burn beneath the spots on her sweater, made the split ends tingle on the nape of her neck. Still, she did not think that he was the type to buy her lunch simply because he felt sorry for her. If it had been pity, he could not have drawn her out as he had done. She had answered his questions because they were so brisk and purposeful. It was as if he had something in mind for her.

She finished her dessert, and set her fork down, and said, "Look, Ray. I wonder if you'd tell me what this is all about now."

He smiled. Her directness did not faze him. "I've been thinking about what you told me. About your situation. Seems to me we've got no variables here. Nothing's going to change unless you change it."

"I see. And you invited me to lunch because you've got a suggestion." She was really curious now. What was he going to recommend to her—a course in computer programming, or an inspirational book by a salesman for Christianity? Neither one seemed quite in character.

"Oh, I got more than a suggestion. I mean, this is Manhattan. Only one reason people go out to lunch here. To talk a deal."

"A deal?"

There was a pause then, as the team of waiters surrounded them, ready to take away the plates and change the tablecloth and refill their coffee cups. Ray caught one man's eye and made a small, definite gesture. Megan thought that they would not be seeing the waiters again for a while.

He leaned back against the banquette, hands on hips, spreading his open jacket from his striped shirtfront. "Whenever I come across someone like you," he said, "I start thinking. I mean, no promises yet, but if the timing's right, if the right people are available, and—most important—if you've got what I hope you've got, I can maybe put something together."

"I see. What do you hope I've got exactly?"

He tapped his brow. "Information."

"Ray, the only thing I know how to do is type."

"There you go running yourself down again. See, I've met a lot of people like you, and I've been able to help them." He paused, choosing among countless examples. "Like for instance, there's my pal Ramona. She used to work in a beauty parlor out on the Island. It's a shitty job, on your feet nine hours a day, slaving over these rich jerks who've got nothing better to do than have their hair done three times a week. Trying to think of new ways to do it, trying to keep 'em happy. And if that's not enough, she had to *listen* to them, too. This sounding familiar, this reminding you of yourself at all?" He grinned and leaned toward her. "Anyway, there's this one who tells Ramona all about this vacation she's got coming up, two weeks in the Greek isles. What does Ramona care? The only isle she's ever gonna see is *Long* Isle. But then she thinks of me. She knows I'm interested in that kind of information."

"I don't understand. What kind of information?"

"Well, that this rich jerk's house in Glen Cove is going to be empty for two weeks."

Megan had a moment of frozen self-consciousness before he spoke again, trying not to show her racing thoughts, trying to hold still and keep the placid expression on her face, as if she were posing for a picture and waiting for the shutter to click.

"See, I know people," he went on, eagerly, earnestly. "Because some of the stuff I handle in the store—not all of it, but some—is hot."

"You're a . . . a . . ."

"Yeah, a fence. As seen on TV."

Megan sat up straight, away from him, and glanced quickly around the restaurant.

"Oh my God," said Ray Klausner, in a stage whisper, "did

anybody hear me? Anybody going to the phone? The cops are going to be here any minute to arrest me—and you too, just because you're talking to me."

Megan laughed out loud. She could not help it—he had guessed her thoughts so exactly.

"Don't worry, the cops know all about me. Sure they hassle me once in a while, but they can be pretty good customers too. Even if their wives have lousy taste in antiques." He was smiling at her, and for the first time since she had met him, he seemed a little shy. "Hey, come on. Hear me out. Maybe you won't go for the deal, but if you don't hear me out I guarantee you'll kick yourself later. You've got to be curious, right?"

Megan's thoughts were slowly catching up with events. "You think that I have information that would help you—"

"I sure do. First step is, you want to pick a good prospect. And you could help with that, couldn't you? I mean, what's a will but a list of the stuff a person owns, right?"

"No. Wrong. I'm afraid you're on the wrong track entirely. You're wasting your time with me." She was looking around for her purse. She found it and put it in her lap, preparing to leave.

"Oh yeah? So set me straight. What's in a will, then?"

"A will isn't specific. Especially a wealthy person's will. It doesn't have lists of furnishings."

"I am way off, then. 'Cause I remember when my Uncle Carl died—this is my rich uncle, you understand—these guys went through the house room by room with a tape recorder. Just like they were making a list."

"Well, they were. The executor will have an inventory made. But that's only for tax purposes, and to save arguments later on. It's a backup. It's not part of the will."

"But it's in the files, right? The files you used to deal with."

Megan did not answer. She was thinking back over those files—over all that paper, all those dry and trivial tasks she used to perform. Ray Klausner was right, though. A man like him could make good use of those files. The realization was so startling that once again she laughed.

Ray laughed with her. "So okay. We're halfway there. We got the house and we know what's in it. All that's left is, when will the people be away?"

61

"Well, that's what I wouldn't know. I hardly ever even meet the people."

"Sure, but you'd hear stuff about them, wouldn't you?"

Megan shook her head. She started to reach for her purse again, and found that it was already in her lap. She had been sitting here listening to this man a little too long. "I'm sorry, you've just got the wrong person."

She started to slide to the edge of the banquette, but Ray leaned urgently toward her. "The wrong person? But you need money, and here's a way to make a lot of it real easy. How come you're the wrong person?"

"Because—because I could never have anything to do with a robbery." She caught herself smiling as she spoke. It was so extraordinary that she should have been brought to say this.

"The thing is, I'm not asking you to. All I'm asking you to do is leak some information. Just give me a tip-off." He gestured southward. "Like the guys on Wall Street do all the time."

"That's different."

"Not really. Sure, they do it all with phones and computers, and in our deal somebody's actually going to have to take some things from one place to another. But that's got nothing to do with you. Don't even think about it." He leaned a little closer, and went on, "Let's take a for-instance, shall we? Let's take this old pal of yours that you told me about."

"Sorry?"

"You know, this rich widow that got you fired. What's her name?"

Megan sat very still. The name Elkin loomed large in her mind. She felt strange. It was as if she'd been standing on a promontory or a high building, enjoying the view, and then had noticed how close she was to the edge, and what a long way down it was. The feeling was the same—that cold tingle in her loins and the pit of her stomach.

"I have to be going now," she muttered, and got to her feet. It took an effort, just as it took an effort to turn away from the view, from the edge.

Ray Klausner sat smiling up at her, looking harmless and unremarkable. "Sure, that's okay. Why don't you take one of my cards, though?"

62

He held the card out to her. Megan shook her head. "No thanks. I don't think I'll be needing it."

"That's true. You know where to find me." He nodded and picked up his coffee cup, and left her to go on her way.

No one looked at her as she walked through the restaurant; but of course there was no reason why anyone should. In another moment she was out again, in the cold air and the indifferent bustle of Third Avenue. She walked to the corner before she even paused to put on her coat, and the pounding of her heart did not begin to ease until she reached the station.

3

Megan had to pause in her typing and lean over for a closer look at an ambiguous scrawl on the purchase order. There was a momentary lull in the others' typing, too, and the radio was not on. At such moments, she could distinctly hear the hum of the electric clock.

It was a large, round, white-faced clock, and it hung upon the wall beside her like the full moon hanging in the night sky. There was nothing else in the office to look at—no pictures, no windows—and it was all too easy to let her eyes be drawn to it. But if she looked once, she would keep on looking, at ever shorter intervals. Each of her glances seemed to weigh upon its hands so that they moved more slowly. She still remembered the day when she had caught a glimpse of the clock at one forty-seven. It had been the longest afternoon of her life.

The lull ended in a renewed clatter of keys. Megan started typing again, too, and forswore checking the time. She was pretty sure that it was almost four thirty—quitting time—but she could not be positive. It was better not to risk disappointment.

Her eyes and fingers worked, as her mind continued to wander. Was it some sort of an initiation rite for the new employee to be placed at this desk, right under the clock? That could be. The other four women in the accounts receivable section had been here for years. They had worked out elaborate protocols about the order of breaks and lunches, the sharing out of each day's quota of purchase orders, and the selection of the radio station. Probably there was a hierarchy to the desks, too. Certainly Pat, the supervisor, sat at the opposite end of the row from Megan.

She came to the end of the form and rolled it out of the typewriter. She began to separate the carbons: white and beige copies into the envelope, for mailing to the customer; blue copy to the shipping department; yellow copy into the tickler file, from which it would resurface a month from today, on December 20, and be sent to the customer as a second demand if he hadn't paid yet; pink copy deeper into the file, to January 20, when, if still unpaid, it was to be given to the supervisor.

December 20 would be almost Christmas. January 20 would be a new year. When those dates came up, she would still be here, filing invoice copies for February and March.

"We've got no variable here," Ray Klausner had said. "Nothing's going to change unless you change it."

Almost a week had passed since her trip to New York. It was all very well to refuse Ray Klausner's card, and tell him she wouldn't consider his offer, but she could not get him out of her mind. She would find that she was recalling what he had said, just as she would sometimes catch herself humming some inane jingle from a commercial. She could hear his offhand, forceful voice, and see his ruddy face before her. While she could not imagine accepting his proposal, she still could not stop thinking about him.

Abruptly a racket of banging drawers and squeaking chairs began around her. Megan turned to look at the clock: four thirty.

As she covered her typewriter her co-workers went past her, calling out their good nights, and by the time she stood up they were already going out the door in a tight, talkative cluster. They were all middle-aged and married, and they had a long drive ahead of them back to their homes in the cheaper suburbs to the north and east. Megan was just as glad she wouldn't have to converse with them on the walk out to the parking lot. They talked very fast, all at the same time, and it was usually about some girl's new hairstyle, or some boy's new car. She could never sort out if it was one of their children they were discussing, or a character in a television series.

As she was putting on her coat she heard a jingle of keys, and the great bulk of Pat the supervisor loomed up beside her. Pat was an immense woman, with a face of such roundness and placidity that her most remarkable feature was her glasses. They had swooping, tusklike sidepieces, and large rectangular lenses, and in the corner of the right one was a small gilt sea-horse. She frequently wondered how Pat could type all day with this mote in her vision; she found her eyes crossing whenever she looked at Pat.

They set off down the corridor together—Megan hugging the wall to make room for Pat's gently swaying bulk—and Pat asked her how she was liking the work.

"Oh, it's all right," was the best Megan could do tonight. Pat asked her this question almost every day, and she was becoming steadily less effusive. She had been so delighted to get this job, after those few terrible days a month ago, and now she could hardly stand it. She wondered if that was something else she had to thank Ray Klausner for, or if it would have happened in any case.

Outside, the evening was fine and brisk. The sun had set but it was not yet dark. Megan longed to be on her own, and she was relieved when they came to Pat's car. It was an old station wagon, with a sticker on the bumper announcing that the car was insured by Smith & Wesson. There was a picture of a gun pointing at the reader.

"Can I give you a lift home?"

"No. I mean, no thanks, it's out of your way. I live down near Shippan."

Pat nodded as she picked through her numerous keys. "You better get that car of yours fixed soon, 'cause soon it'll be dark when we get out of work."

In fact there was nothing wrong with Megan's car except that she had decided she couldn't afford the insurance premium. This fiction that the car was in the shop was getting to be more trouble to maintain than it was worth. "I will," she said, turning away. "Good night."

"See you Monday," said Pat. She always had to say it.

Megan set out striding fast, taking deep breaths of the chilly air. The first part of her walk was along a featureless street of gas stations and auto parts stores, so she passed the time with thinking about the pleasures of the evening before her: kicking off her shoes and putting her feet up to watch the news, having a glass of wine—two glasses, since it was Friday. Then she would dine on a bowl of soup and read for as long as she pleased.

She came to the corner of Shippan Avenue. It was a bad intersection, where four busy roads met at odd angles. There was no pedestrian signal, and she always had to wait for her chance to cross. She did not like waiting at this corner, because only half a mile farther down, Shippan Avenue crossed Shady Lane. She could not get over the feeling that one day, as she stood poised on the curb, one of the cars that went whizzing by her would be a green Saab, and it would be Paul, on his way to see Mrs. Elkin. It did not happen this evening, though. The light changed. She hurried across and continued on her way.

She wondered how long it would take before she would stop expecting to see Paul. Selling his presents, rooting him out of her apartment, had not helped. Her imagination, wily and tireless, kept conjuring him up. When her phone rang once and then relapsed into its usual silence, she would think that it was Paul. Not somebody who realized he had dialed wrong, not an electronic glitch, but Paul, who had started to call her and then changed his mind. When she reasoned these imaginings away, though, she would feel so alone. She would feel that she had slipped through a crack in life, and would never get back.

She left the busy street behind her and came to a pleasant

block of neat, small houses. Their lights were just coming on, and the blue glow of television shone through their front windows. She crossed another street, and the neighborhood slipped a notch. This was a short block of shabby, huddled bungalows. She had to walk down the middle of the street, because there were no sidewalks, and both curbs were solidly lined with vehicles: pickup trucks perched on gigantic tires, rusty old Cadillacs, muscle cars with gleaming, swooping hoods. This was her street, and the featureless three-story building at the end of it was her home.

The stairwell was filled with the smells of other people's cooking. She climbed the steps to her apartment and let herself in. Sinking down on the sofa, she took off her shoes. A weariness came over her. Just now she did not feel like getting her wine or putting the soup on to warm. She lay back and listened to the noises coming through the walls.

Early evening was one of the times of day when her apartment would fill up with ghostly sounds: indistinct voices, the rush of water through pipes, the tinny murmur of a television set. She could hear footfalls too—not from the stairwell but from the back fire escape. So it was probably one of the neighbors, coming upstairs. For a moment she allowed herself to hope that he was coming to see her. She did not know any of her neighbors except to say hello to them, but every once in a while somebody would drop by to borrow a kitchen utensil, or change for the washing machine. That would be an event in her long night, and she listened intently as the sound of the footfalls changed: whoever it was had reached her landing. She waited for the sound to change again as he started up the next flight. But instead he stopped, and knocked on her door.

She had a moment of being pleasantly flustered, putting on her shoes and smoothing her hair. Then she dashed into the kitchen, flipped on the light, and opened the door.

It was not one of the neighbors but a short, stocky boy. Light shone on the blond top of his head. He was carrying something, and she thought he must be a delivery boy gone astray.

"Hi, how you doin'?"

"All right."

He held up a couple of bags. "I got your stuff here."

They were the plastic shopping bags she had left in Ray Klausner's office. She had written them off the moment she noticed their absence. She doubted that Ray would take the trouble to return them to her. But apparently he was willing to take more trouble over her than she had thought.

She reached through the gap in the door. "Oh, thanks. Thank you very much." But he put his hands behind his back. "Uh-uh. You want your stuff back, you got to let me in. I mean, I came all the way up here. You got to let me talk for a minute."

He stood, head thrown back, grinning—she could see the faint glimmer of his teeth in the dark shape of his face. He was daring her. Megan did not take dares. Not usually. But now she had another of those moments when she stepped back and regarded herself with amazement. Was she really going to mumble an apology and shut the door, sacrificing her belongings, then go back to the couch in the dark empty room, and spend the next hour wondering why she had been so frightened of this boy?

No, she was not.

"All right," she said. "I'll give you a minute." She stepped back.

He went past her to the counter and laid the bags down. It was only a few steps, but he managed to put a lot of swagger into them. His blond hair was pulled back into a tight pigtail, in the style of the young punks she saw at the mall, and he had on a suede jacket with a lot of belts and zippers, tight jeans, and gaudy running shoes with belts instead of laces.

She thought he must be some obstreperous nephew of Ray Klausner's. "Did Ray send you here?"

"Not exactly. He don't figure you for a hot prospect. But I figured I'd give you a try." He leaned back against the refrigerator, sturdy legs braced, shoulders planted as if in an invisible niche. Now that she could see his face in full light she realized she had been wrong about his age. He was younger than she, but he was not a teenager. When he brushed his blond forelock back, his pale blue eyes looked hard and tired, and there was a grimness about his mouth: long grooves ran from his nostrils to its corners, and his philtrum was as deep and sharp-edged as a gutter.

"Who are you? You work for Ray, don't you?"

"My name's Steve. And I don't work *for* him. Only if you was to spot a house for him, I'd be the one to do the job."

It took her a moment to catch the meaning. Then, instinctively, she dropped her eyes, and found she was looking at his gaudy running shoes. But of course, she thought giddily, a burglar would have good sneakers.

"Old Klausner, he forgot to tell you the most important part. How we cut up the score. It's going to be a fifty-fifty split. How 'bout that? I'm the one that goes in there and gets all the stuff out, and you get as much as I do. Just for talking."

He grinned at her, shaking his head. He seemed to feel that the chance to get the better of him was something no one could resist.

"It's no use," Megan replied. "I've already told Ray. You've simply got the wrong person."

"Yeah, how come?" He waited, and when she did not answer, he went on, "You've been thinking about it. You don't have to tell me that, I know. So what you been thinking?"

"There's no use thinking about it. Even if I went along with you, even if it worked, I know I couldn't—couldn't live with myself afterward."

It was hard to get out the last words. They were true—at least she thought they were true—but she felt awkward and foolish when she was brought to say them.

Steve said, "So you're doing fine living with yourself now, huh?"

"What?"

"See, this is what I don't get. How you can go around knowing somebody owes you. This rich old bag, she fucked up your old life. Don't you figure she owes you a start on a new one?"

"I don't think that way. I'm not a—a vengeful person."

"Good," Steve said. "Glad to hear it. 'Cause you couldn't get back at her, even if you want to. She's rich. You know what happens when somebody rich gets robbed? All their rich jerk friends and family come around and they say, 'Oh you poor dear. What a shame. The scum who did this ought to be burned alive!' " Steve paused and smiled dreamily. "You know, all the stuff that makes a person feel better. And then they go off to some fucking spa to get over the shock, and when they get back, the insurance man is waiting with the check. She's insured up to the eyeballs, right?"

"Yes," Megan said. "As a matter of fact she is."

Steve's blue eyes were brighter, more avid, seeing that she knew this. "So what have you done to her? You made her go shopping for some new stuff. What's that compared to what she did to you? So like I say, don't do it to get back at her. Do it for money."

"What good would the money be to me? How could I explain where I got it?"

"Explain to who? Who's gonna ask? Nobody gives a shit about you now, right? So who's gonna ask?" He dug a pack of cigarettes out of his pocket and lit one. "What you do is, you move to the city or to Boston. Not that you have to, but who'd want to hang around this lousy town? You set yourself up the way you like. The people you meet, you tell 'em you got divorced, and you decided to take your half of the property settlement, move someplace new and make a fresh start. Lots of girls do that these days."

Megan had listened intently to what he'd said. It had a plausibility that drew her despite herself. Bright, indistinct things—possibilities—flurried across her mind, and something strong and warm seemed to pass round her, like a wave in a warm sea, lifting her for a moment, gently letting her down. It was hope.

There was a sudden whistling torrent in the pipes behind the wall: her neighbors were washing dishes, as they did this time every evening. Here I am in my kitchen, discussing a burglary, Megan thought. Everything seemed bizarre yet inconsequential, as in a dream one knows is a dream. She said, "What is it exactly that you would need to know?" and the words went out into the air and hung there, as if she could call them back if she wanted to, but she didn't want to.

Steve drew on his cigarette. "Most important thing is, I got to know when the house is gonna be empty. And that means one whole night at least when there's nobody home, and nobody coming home. 'Cause the way I am when I'm on a job, I hear a sound and I'm out the window. Head-first. Even if it's the second floor."

He was grinning again, but Megan shook her head in perplexity. "But this woman—she has three kids and a live-in governess. And I don't know anything about their day-to-day movements. I never did, and I've been completely cut off for a month now."

"I'm not talking about day-to-day. Like, rich people don't stay home all winter. Don't they go south in February, March, somewhere along in there?"

"They go to Florida every year, but I don't know when. It all depends on the kids' school vacations."

"Okay. Let's stick to dates we know about then. How 'bout Christmas? They go over the river and through the woods to granny's or something?"

"No, they're all home then. The house is full up."

"How about Thanksgiving?"

"Thanksgiving?" Megan had been leaning against the counter. Now, unconsciously, she put her hands flat behind her and pushed herself upright. The Elkins had a Thanksgiving ritual that had remained fixed and unalterable for as long as she had known of them. They would be at an uncle's, in New York, not at Shady Lane. The house was going to be empty, six nights from tonight.

"Oh no," she breathed. "That's too soon."

Her heart began to beat heavily and quickly. She had to move, so she started pacing along the far wall of the kitchen, her arms folded over her middle as if she were cold.

"So," Steve said. "It's Thanksgiving."

She halted with her back to him. "Wait just a minute. You and Ray, you keep talking as if this isn't what it is. Isn't a crime. But I know—"

"Hey, that's just Klausner you're talking about. Not me. Did he give you his big routine, how what we're doing is no different from what the guys on Wall Street do all the time?"

He had dropped into a perfect imitation of Ray's ebullient, knowing voice. "Yes," she said, "that's the routine he gave me."

"Well, no wonder he didn't get anywhere with you. You're smart. You know the difference. The guys on Wall Street, if they screw up they don't go to the joint. You and me would. See, Klausner doesn't give a shit, but I'm the one that's going in the house, and I'm gonna be scared. You ought to be scared too."

Megan said, "I'm scared, all right."

He gave another of his broad but fleeting grins and leaned over to flick ash in the sink. "Okay. We got that settled. Now do you go for it or not? There's nothing I can say. Whether the job's gonna be a cinch or a fuck-up, that depends on you, on your information. You can judge better than me." He took a drag on the cigarette and waited. When she said nothing, he went on. "If you can tell me about the layout of the place, so I know what I'm looking for and where to find it, I can make it a real quick job. The less time I'm in there, the safer it is. Then if you could tell me something about the locks and alarms, so I won't have any trouble there . . . like I say, it's up to you. See what you can find out, then make up your mind."

"It would be in the file," said Megan slowly. "All of it. But the file's at the firm."

"At your old office, you mean? Then maybe you could get it."

"Oh sure. Just walk in and ask for it?"

Steve took another thoughtful drag on his cigarette. "I don't guess you got a key to the place. I mean, I guess they took it back from you?"

The question threw Megan for a moment. A key had been issued to her—what had happened to it? Arthur Lasch wouldn't have asked for it when he fired her, for partners were above such details. Since her departure had been so abrupt, there had been no time for the usual formalities. The key must still be in the pocket of her briefcase. She murmured, "I suppose I've still got it."

Steve chuckled and slowly shook his head. "Jesus, lady, I don't know. When luck is behind you, pushing like that, maybe you ought to go for it."

"I'm not sure I could go back there."

He made a small sound that could have been a laugh or a sigh. "It's not just the cops, is it? You're scared of being scared."

"Yes," she said. "I guess that's it."

"Well, don't feel bad. It's what stops most people. It's the only thing that stops most people." He straightened up and flicked his cigarette butt into the sink, where it hissed and went out. "What they don't know is, making a score feels good."

"I suppose it does, when you've gotten away with it. When you have the money and you're safe."

"I'm not talking about that. I mean when you're doing it you're real high. All you have to do, you say to yourself, 'Fuck 'em. I'm going for it.' And you start to feel great right away. I can't, like, explain it to you. You just got to do it to find out."

He was heading for the door now, zipping up his jacket. Megan started to say, "Wait—"

"Nah, we talked enough. You decide to do it, you know where to find Klausner."

He nodded to her and left, as if they were two strangers who'd been chatting on a bus.

4

The next morning Megan awakened slowly from a troubled sleep. She had dreamt a complex, hectic dream that was somehow about Paul. But she could not remember the details, and it was fading with each second she was awake.

There was a click from the bedside table. It was the noise her digital clock made when a new numeral fell into place. She had grown unused to the noise while the clock had not been there. It had been one of the things she had left at the Raymond Gallery.

Last night, after Steve had gone, she had restored all the things he'd brought back to their usual places. She had done other things, too, in the course of that long, restless evening: dug her briefcase out of the closet and taken from it the office key and the magnetic card that gave access to the building. She had also worked it out that if she was going into the firm, this morning was the time to do it.

There was never a time when she could be certain that the office would be empty. A law firm was in the business of selling expertise by the hour, and younger associates were always complaining boastfully about their all-nighters and their weekends at their desks. But the early hours of Saturday morning offered the best chance. It was rare for anyone to work through Friday night, and people who came in on Saturday did not begin to arrive until nine or ten. She would never have a better opportunity than now.

She heard another click from the bedside table as another minute passed. Perhaps she had slept too long and it was too late to go in today. She turned her head and looked. The clock said 6:47.

So there was still time.

Megan rolled her head back and shut her eyes. That won't do any good, she told herself. You'll still hear the clicks. If you lie here until it's too late, you'll have to hear every minute pass and be lost. She thought of that other clock she dared not look at, the bland, humming clock on the wall of the office. All she did was wait while clocks took her life away. She felt a flash of impatience—really felt it, as something hot and tearing below her breastbone. The joints of her arms and legs tensed. She was not going to be here when the next digit fell into place. She threw the covers off and got out of bed.

Outside, the pavement was wet and black beneath a gray sky. She felt the chilly prickle of raindrops on her head and the backs of her hands. It was the sort of light, steady drizzle that would soak her to the skin by the time she got downtown. Digging in her pockets for keys, she walked down the row of cars until she came to her own.

It was almost two weeks since she had driven the car. The battery would probably be dead. But when she turned the key,

74

the starter ground weakly. She coaxed the engine into life, with the skill born of long practice. She'd had this car for many years, and it had been old when she bought it. She wondered what it would be like to have a new car.

Switching on the lights and wipers, she pulled away from the curb. Before she was out of second gear she had reached the corner, and in another few moments she was approaching the intersection where she had to wait so long on her walks home. The traffic signal was flashing long yellow streaks down the empty pavement, and she drove straight through. Now the gas stations and auto parts stores were unfurling past her windows in a blur. The rain beat harmlessly against the windshield, and the drops were swept away by the wipers. Ahead, the stunted skyscrapers of downtown stood out dull silver against the tumbled gray clouds. She would be there in a couple of minutes. She had lost her sense of how quickly you could get around in a car, and it exhilarated her. What had Steve said, last night?—you had only to decide to go for it, and you would start to feel better. And he was right. She did feel better, even though she had not yet taken the first step. She hadn't even broken a law yet.

But no—in the state of Connecticut it was illegal to drive without insurance, and hers had lapsed. I've crossed the line already, she said to herself, and the thought was so melodramatic that she laughed aloud.

Habit prompted her to turn on the street that led to the garage entrance, but there would be an attendant on duty there, and she did not want to be seen by any more people than necessary. Instead she drove around to the front of the building and parked on the street. Leaving the car, she climbed the steps that led to the bank of glass doors. There was no need for the card-key; a door was open.

She walked across the lobby. There was a security guard sitting at the desk. He glanced up from his newspaper. His face was vaguely familiar to her, as hers must be to him. She prepared to nod and smile as she drew near him, but he had already turned his attention back to the paper.

Now for the visitors' book. It rested on a rostrum in front of the row of elevators. She picked up the chained pen and held it over the page. This was just in case the guard was watching her, for of course she could not sign in. It was easy to pantomime a signature. She had only to hold her hand over the page and allow it to tremble.

All the elevators were waiting, doors open. She stepped into the nearest one and ascended without a stop to the eleventh floor. Up there it was so quiet that she could hear the elevator going down as she walked to the firm's double doors. The click of the key in the lock echoed loudly down the hall.

She closed the door behind her and stood still for a moment, listening. Apart from the sigh of the ventilators there was not a sound. Nobody was here. She crossed the dark lobby and went through to the offices. The corridor was dim, illumined only by the weak daylight. She walked past Paul's closed door and Arthur Lasch's open one, and came to her old cubicle at the end of the hall. But no nameplate had replaced hers in the bracket, and the office looked unused. The Elkin file would be in Paul's office, then.

She opened the door and switched on the light. For a moment she stood still, waiting for the wave of emotion to hit her. Only last night the prospect of catching a glimpse of him driving past had seemed so momentous; surely she ought to feel something now that she was here. But there was so little of Paul in the room. He had not decorated it with his own personal furniture, the way the other partners did. He hadn't hung the walls with his license and diplomas, his citations and awards. There was only a line of color photographs—expensively mounted, quite conventional shots: a waterfall sparkling through mist, a still-bright maple leaf encased in ice. Megan did not look at these. She knew them well. She had been shivering beside him when he clicked the shutter.

She went around the desk, sat in his chair, and swiveled to the file cabinet. The fat leatherette envelope of folders marked Elkin was there. She hauled it out, rested it on her knees. There was nowhere to put it on the cluttered desk. Paul had disordered the file, too—he generated mess as he worked. There was no need to put things back exactly as she had found them, for he'd never notice. As she took what she wanted, that strange, cool exhilaration arose in her again.

Leaving the files open on the desk she went down the hall to the copying room and switched on the machine. The humming and clunking it made as she fed the papers through seemed very loud in the silent office. Her nerves began to stir again. Waiting for the copies to slide out, she had to struggle to keep from turning and looking toward the door. Don't bother, it's pointless, she told herself. If there is someone there, it's too late. She would already have been discovered, and she would only seem more furtive if she was looking over her shoulder when she was caught. Anyway, the office was empty, and would be for hours. But as the last page was running through the machine, she could resist no longer. She turned and looked, and there was someone standing in the doorway.

Megan flinched violently, an all-too-visible spasm of the limbs. Her mind went blank.

"Meg? Sorry. I didn't mean to . . . um . . . startle you."

The sound of the voice was a release. She looked again at the figure, which in her first panic had been faceless. Now she could recognize the woman's big blue eyes, bruised with smeared makeup, her small mouth and fleshy chin. It was Heather, one of the litigation paralegals. She was wearing a hat with drooping brim and a wet coat: she must just have come in.

She had said something—what was it? She had apologized. So Megan said, "It's okay. I just wasn't expecting anyone."

"I had to pick up some files for Goldman. He's got a deposition today." The lips compressed. "Meg, what are you doing here?"

Even as Megan drew in a long breath to answer, she did not know what she was going to say. But then it came out, clearly and easily. "I'm copying some things I worked on. For a work sample to show at interviews. See, I'm looking for another legal assistant job."

Heather's face softened in comprehension and sympathy. "Oh, right, they like to see those. So how's it been going for you, Meg? Did you manage to find some kind of job to—you know, to tide you over?"

As Megan turned the pages face down and gathered them up, they chatted about her job at the Kel-Dro Corporation. All the while, she was marveling at her own swift inventiveness. What she'd said had been the perfect lie. For Heather was an officer of the local paraprofessional association, and in trying to recruit Megan months before she had given her that tip about work samples. Megan had remembered. She had even remembered that Heather was one of those who professed to find a shade more dignity in the term "legal assistant" than in "paralegal." But then, all her life Megan had been striving to say the things that would please people, so it was no surprise that she should turn out to be a good liar.

With the copies in her pocket and the originals clasped to her breast, she advanced on Heather. "Well, I won't keep you. Nice seeing you again."

She stepped back. "Oh sure, Meg. Good luck."

Heather would see her go into Paul's office, she realized. But that was all right, because most of the files she had worked on were there. She set about her task: papers back in order, staple, return to the file. She forced herself not to hurry, even when she saw Heather appear in the doorway. The woman said nothing, but she hovered and looked expectant. Perhaps she did suspect something. Megan finished her work and raised her head.

Heather advanced a few tentative steps. She said, "You know, Paul's spending all his time in here these days."

"But this is his office," said Megan, confused.

"Sure, but I mean all the time. He comes in early and stays late, and just works in here with the door closed. He doesn't even show up at the Friday hospitality hours. Pam says he's like—depressed."

Megan could not think what to say. She remembered now that the Elkin will construction hearing was coming up—the court date she had secured as one of her last services for him was coming up in two weeks. Then Paul would have to stand up in court and tell the judge that he had made a mistake in the will. Even if he could blame most of it on his ex-paralegal, he would still have to admit that he had made a mistake, and nothing could be more distasteful to him. Of course he would be moody—and Heather and the other paralegals would make the most of it. They studied the lawyers' tones and facial expressions as intently as dogs study their masters', and they were prone to exaggerate. A childish snit was elevated into a heroic rage. Mild preoccupation became dark brooding. No doubt this was what had happened with Paul. She shrugged and said, "I guess he's got something on his mind."

"Well, yeah, but he's been that way ever since you got— since you left." Heather took another step forward. A deep flush suffused her round cheeks, and even though they were all alone in the suite of offices, she dropped her voice. "I know it's none of my business, but you and him were kind of involved, weren't you?"

Megan looked down and put a hand to her brow. She wasn't confident of being able to control her expression. This was too rich. That after he had dropped her in such a businesslike way, Paul should be suspected of such sentimentality. It was really too bad for him. He had taken so many precautions, and forced so many humiliations on her, to keep this secret, and in the end—after the end—he had betrayed it himself. He was exposed. For if Heather knew, everyone knew.

The woman took a step nearer. The demure blush did nothing to soften the avidity of her eyes. She had been watching, and was gratified with what she saw. "That's why you came in so early, right? 'Cause you wanted to be real sure— *real* sure—you wouldn't meet up with Paul?"

Megan put the file back in the drawer and slid it home. She stood, and took a deep breath and let it out. A sigh, Heather was going to call it.

"I suppose I'd just as soon not see Paul again."

Then, quickly, keeping her head down, she left the office and hurried down the corridor. All the way she could feel Heather's gaze upon her back. Megan hoped that one of the other paralegals would be in soon; she didn't want poor Heather to have to hold in this wonderful story for too long. This perfect coda to the tale of Megan Lofting. Her place in the firm lore was secure now.

A moment later she emerged from the building. The cool, damp air was oddly bracing, and she skipped down the steps and dashed across the street to her car. It didn't matter what they said about that Megan Lofting, the old one. That sad figure who had crept into the firm in order to avoid a painful meeting with her ex-lover. She was leaving that person behind, right here, to be useful to her. When there was such a titillating motive for her conduct, who would look for another? Her real purpose was as safe as if she had never been seen at all.

She hesitated once she was behind the wheel. She hadn't thought beyond the first daunting step, perhaps believing she'd never get this far. But there was not much time, and she had better get on with it.

She drove the block to the turnpike and mounted the ramp beneath the sign that read SOUTH—NY CITY.

Third Avenue was virtually empty at that early hour, and the windows of the Raymond Gallery were dark behind their steel gates. But her ring brought someone to show her back to Ray's office, and in a few minutes the man himself appeared. He showed no surprise on seeing her here. He was busy, but no less hospitable for that. She was provided with a comfortable chair in which to wait, magazines, and a cup of astringent black coffee. The hall outside the door resounded with footsteps and shouts, thumps and bangs. A truck in the alley out back was being unloaded. It occurred to her that this was the haul from a burglary being brought in. They were no more surreptitious about their task than garbage men.

Eventually Ray returned. He sank heavily into the chair opposite her and said, "Okay, I'm all yours."

"This Wednesday is the night to do it."

"Tell me."

Megan hesitated a moment, feeling the lack of Ray Klausner's former effusiveness. He sat slumped in the chair, his eyes flat, his face seemingly a less vivid hue than before. Then she realized that his vitality seemed low simply because he was not doing a selling job on her anymore. The sale was made, the deal done: she was here, wasn't she?

"There's an uncle, the late husband's brother. He's a widower, with a big apartment on Central Park West. Every year, they go down there to watch the Macy's Thanksgiving Day parade from the terrace."

"So when's she leave, and when's she get back?"

"They'll go on Wednesday, to miss the traffic. As soon as the kids get home from school. They'll probably stay through the weekend. At least through Friday. She takes them shopping on Fifth Avenue. She said once that if she doesn't give them a few presents to tide them over, they won't give her a moment's peace until Christmas."

"Well, of course. If you're a rich kid you deserve Christmas at least twice a year." He showed his familiar grin for the first time, but then it faded. "One thing, though. We go Wednesday night, that doesn't give me much time. I got a lot of calls to make."

"Calls?" Odd how familiar this is, Megan thought: it was like buying a car, that moment when the salesman had your interest hooked, and began to talk about financing.

"Yeah. That's the way I work. See, when you're well-known in the trade, like I am, you got people coming in all the time, saying, Ray, keep an eye out for so-and-so for me, will you? So as soon as I know what I'm going to have on hand, I start making calls. I got a lot of the stuff sold before it even comes in. May even have the whole haul moved through the store before the job's even reported to the cops. Better for me, better for everybody that way." He leaned forward, elbows on knees, and fixed his eyes gravely on hers. "So I better get going right away. That the inventory you got there?"

He held out his hand, glancing at the sheaf of photocopies in her lap. Megan put her hand over them. She had been expecting something like this. She had always tried hard to anticipate what other people would do, she had always been obliging. That was something else she was finished with. She said, "I have a couple of questions first."

Ray leaned back. "Ask away."

"How long will I have to wait for my money?"

"You don't wait at all. We do the job Wednesday night, you come down here Thursday, I pay you. Cash. I've got no problem with front money, because I move things so fast, like I said."

"And once I show you the inventory, you can tell me what I'm going to get?"

Ray was shaking his head. "No. Sorry. I'm not going to bullshit you, and that's all it would be. Too much we don't know yet. Like, some rich people leave a lot of cash lying around. Others, they put it on American Express or have somebody else pick up the tab, and you don't find a dime in their houses. Or take jewelry. If it's in the dresser drawers, fine. If it's in a safe, not so good. 'Cause Steve ain't exactly Raffles the amateur cracksman. Oriental rugs, same thing. How big, how much furniture is he going to have to move to get them up? 'Cause he ain't the Mayflower moving company, either. And then, like I say, I got to make the calls, do the haggling. I'll get the best deal I can for us, trust me."

"That was my other question," Megan said. "How do I know that I can trust you?"

She expected him to be either indignant or amused. But he answered matter-of-factly. "Because I want to stay on good terms with you. Because there's more where that came from, right?"

He gestured again at the photocopies. Megan tried not to show her astonishment. If looking ahead to the next job would keep him honest, she should let him do so. So she stifled the urge to cry out, do you think I would ever do this again? Do you think I would ever do it to anyone who hadn't harmed me first?

Ray Klausner was stretching out his hand again. "Well, if there's nothing else . . ."

She gave him the papers. He unfolded the sheaf and began to read.

"That's a room-by-room inventory, done at the time of Mr.—" She hesitated, remembering how a week ago Ray had tried and failed to get the name out of her. But it was on the top of every page and so was the address on Shady Lane. "Of Mr. Elkin's death, last summer," she finished.

Ray didn't hear her. He was making a quick, intent study of the inventory. She was reminded of the way the sharp, experienced lawyers at Goldman Lasch used to go through contracts: that savvy, that knowing what to look for. After a few moments he rose and shoved the thick sheaf of papers into his back pocket. "We're all going to do real well off of this. Real well. See you Thursday. Payday. Make it early, though, I got to get to my relatives' by four."

Taken by surprise, she got up too. "That's it?"

"You're all done. Easy, huh?"

He was opening the door. As she stepped through it she saw Steve, waiting in the hallway. He must have been waiting a long time. He was sagging against the wall, his body hanging from his shoulderblades like a coat from a hook. Now he straightened up and looked from one to the other, registering the fact that he had been left outside while they talked.

"Hey, I told you. Told you she'd show up."

"Yeah," Ray said. He was looking down the hall, toward the loading dock at the back.

"Told you I'd get her here."

"Yeah, yeah. Go on in. I got a few things to take care of." He nodded to Megan and turned away. Steve looked after him. There was more emotion in his face than she had seen before. It was the look of unsurprised disappointment that wretched children gave their parents.

She turned to go back to the street, but Steve stepped in her way. "Hey. You bring the stuff on the alarms, like I asked for?"

"Yes. I copied a page from the insurance forms. Ray has it." She turned away again, but he stepped in front of her. She had the feeling he needed to re-assert his importance, now she had seen him slighted by Ray Klausner.

"One more thing. Be at the train station. Not Stamford, the station before Stamford, whatever it is. Noon on Tuesday. I want to do a drive-by."

She recoiled from the demand. "I can't drive you by the house. I have to work."

"So we make it early. Eight A.M."

"Ray's got the forms. I don't see what else you need."

"Is it in the forms whether they got streetlights on this block? What kinds of trees around the house—evergreens, or the kind that don't got no leaves? How far to the house next door? The one across the street? Or maybe you can tell me this. The driveway blacktop or gravel?"

"I—I don't know."

"Then we do a drive-by. Gravel sounds real loud under your tires at three in the morning." He turned and went into the office.

Megan felt the familiar quivering tightness inside her. Only this time, she knew, it would not go away. She would have to live with it for every instant of the next four days. The burglary was no longer a tantalizing possibility, a chance not to be missed. It was real. It was going to happen.

5

On Monday evening, Megan was walking home from the public library. It was not cold, but a damp, penetrating wind was blowing. She looked up at the dun-colored sky and quickened her pace, hoping to get home before the rain started. She had gone back to walking again, because walking took up more time.

She had stayed in the library until closing time. It was late. There was no one else on the brightly lit sidewalks, and only an occasional car went rushing past in the street. Gradually, over the buzz of the street lamps, she became aware of a strange noise, a deep, regular booming. It was getting louder: she was heading for it.

Presently she rounded the corner of an office building and came upon the source of the noise. It was a demolition site where work was going on all night. She saw, over a hoarding and through a gap between old buildings, men and vehicles moving in the glare and black shadows of big lights. She could not see the headache ball that was making the noise, but she could feel each impact through the soles of her shoes, and hear the tumbling of stone and rubble that followed each crash. She turned and walked on. It was a long time before the sound faded behind her.

There was something surreptitious about this night work, as if an act of vandalism on a giant scale were being committed when no one was around. In fact, Stamford was enjoying a construction boom so feverish that sometimes it did look perversely like a city that was being razed. The illusion seemed especially strong to Megan tonight. Passing a huge, fenced-in hole in the ground, she thought it could as well have been a bomb crater as the foundation for a new building. When she came upon the steel framework of a rising skyscraper, it looked to her as frail and bare as a skeleton.

She continued to play with this idea as she walked along. Suppose those clattering jackhammers and snarling bulldozers that one heard all day long were actually tearing the place down? Suppose those many-wheeled dump trucks that prowled the streets were hauling Stamford away, bit by bit? She shook her head and smiled to herself. When you were about to leave a place forever, you could easily imagine that it would cease to exist, that the place, not you, was the transient.

She turned a corner, into a long narrow slot of a road which ran between a row of blank-walled parking structures and the concrete flank of the elevated turnpike. She looked up at the cars and trucks whizzing past on the highway she was intending to take out of here.

She had decided that this evening, after spending hours in the library, hunched over a road atlas of the United States, tracing routes west. There were other choices: you could go north from Stamford and take I-86 across the Mid-Hudson Bridge. That would get you out of the traffic and the suburban sprawl as quickly as possible. But I-95 was the more direct route, and she had decided that it would be the more satisfying as well. She would get on the turnpike at her usual entrance ramp, then drive south past the plush familiar suburbs. One last time she would pick her way through the labyrinthine ruins of the Bronx. Manhattan would be a momentary flurry of tunnels and signs, and then she would shoot out onto the George Washington Bridge. Then the marshes and refineries of New Jersey. At last the traffic would begin to thin out, and the land to rise, and she would be in the wooded passes of the Delaware Water Gap.

This was about as far as Megan could go in visualizing her trip. She had never crossed the Pennsylvania border, never seen any other part of the country, except for long-ago trips to Florida and Los Angeles. It had filled her with wonder and impatience to look at the map. Here was this far corner of the nation where she had spent her whole life, a dense thicket of roads and place names crammed hard against the edge of the sea, and here were the bold green slashes of the Interstates, running west or south. Trace any one with a finger, and the names and the roads dwindled, the big country opened up.

With a giddy resolve she had fixed upon Santa Fe as her destination. She liked what she had read about it—the clean dry air, the long vistas of desert and mountain, mesa and arroyo. She wasn't sure what an arroyo was, but she was eager to find out. And it was a sensible choice, a small city, but one where she would blend in easily. Santa Fe, she gathered from her reading, was a place that people like herself went to—Easterners with a bit of money, looking for a new life.

The people you meet, Steve had said, you tell them you got divorced and you decided to take your half of the property settlement and move someplace new and start over. Lots of women do that these days. Megan had embraced this new past, and whiled away the hours filling in details. It was Paul, of course, who was her "ex." It would be easy for her to speak of him in that tone of muted, puzzled bitterness that so many divorced women fell into when speaking of their former husbands. She could even imagine the house that had been sold in order to fund this new life of hers. This alternative past was much more pleasant to think about than what had actually been done to her, and what she was taking part in. She knew that if she doted on it for long enough, alone in the new car on the long drive west, she would come to accept it as her own.

She walked beneath the dank turnpike and railroad underpasses. The skyscrapers were behind her now, and she had only to walk that long street of darkened gas stations to get home. Out of habit she crossed the street. There was a fire station a few blocks away, and she always gave it a wide berth. Sirens and uniforms made her think of the police.

A few dark spots were appearing on the pavement. She felt a stinging raindrop on her bare head and quickened her pace. The wind was picking up. Branches rattled against buildings; dead leaves skittered behind her like footsteps. Megan's nerves began to draw taut. It always happened at about this time, when she was trying to relax for bed, hoping that she would be able to get some sleep.

The signal at the next corner changed and a small pack of cars came at her. She averted her eyes from the dazzling headlights. Then she heard the squeak of tires as one of the cars swerved into the street behind her and braked to a stop. She flinched and began to walk even faster. She had gone several paces before she realized that someone was calling her name. She turned. It was Paul.

She had not recognized the shouting voice, but she knew the dark, indistinct figure from the way he moved as he got out of the car. Then he was running toward her, running flat-out, arms pumping and the tails of his coat flying, as if she were fleeing from him. But she was only standing and waiting, numb with surprise.

He came to a lurching stop before her. "Meg. I thought it was you. What are you doing out so late? Alone?"

"I was . . . I was just walking home."

"But it's raining." He held up a cupped hand, as if it were necessary to catch some rain and show it to her. "Good thing I came along. I'll give you a ride."

"But you're going the other way."

"A classic Megan Lofting response." He bowed his head, chuckling. She gazed at the raindrops glittering in his dark hair. This is Paul, she thought, it really is. She realized she had not looked at him until now. She had been avoiding his eyes. When he raised his head again, she thought that he did not look well. No doubt that was just the flat greenish glare from the street-lamps.

"Look, I don't mind running you home. The hardship of going a couple of blocks out of my way is one that I can bear. Okay?"

He took her arm—awkwardly, like a teenage boy who was eager for the excuse to touch her, and they walked back to the car. Paul was taller than she and his stride was longer. When she walked with him, she always had to lengthen her step. It felt very strange, now, to be doing that again.

And here was the green Saab, its engine idling deferentially. The door closed behind her with the familiar solid *thunk*. The seat—her seat—was as comfortable as ever. Her feet bumped against objects on the floor, which she knew would be an umbrella and a squash racket.

He got in beside her but did not put the car in gear. She glanced over, to see that he was slowly shaking his head. "I don't know what I'm trying to pull here. You wouldn't really let me get away with this, would you?"

"What?"

"Look, I didn't just happen along. I've been at your apartment."

"My apartment?"

"Well, your street. I've been sitting in the car all evening waiting for you. I'd just given up . . ." He paused for a moment. The jocularity had drained abruptly from his voice. "No, that's not true. I was going to get a cup of coffee and go back. I had to see you, Meg. Just had to."

He turned to her now, and she turned away. "Why?" she asked.

He gestured in the darkness. "Look, was this some sort of contest, to see who could wait who out? If it was, you win. I broke down first. You win."

"What do I win?"

"Huh?"

"I said, what do I win?"

He let out his breath, reached for the wheel and the gear lever. "A ride home, I guess."

The car pulled out onto the street and accelerated. It's only a few blocks, Megan told herself, only a couple of minutes and he'll be gone. But the damage was done already. Her body was rigidly alert; her thoughts roiling. It was going to take hours to get to sleep tonight.

"Look. Obviously I've started off on the wrong note here. I came to see you because I think about you all the time. I had to know how you're doing. You can understand that, can't you?"

"You've managed to live with your curiosity for a long time."

Paul was very still then. Her corner was coming up, but instead of braking he stepped on the gas. The street flashed by.

"You missed the turn. You'll have to go back."

88

"Not yet. I have to talk to you, and somehow I get the feeling that you're not planning to invite me in."

She flung out an arm to brace herself against the dashboard. It seemed to her they were hurtling through the empty streets. "Stop this car. Let me out."

He slowed down, but did not stop. "Megan, we are going to talk. I've been waiting for you for two and a half hours tonight. And it's not as if tonight is the first time."

"I don't know what that's supposed to mean."

"When I brought your stuff back. I waited around for I don't know how long. And that was a Sunday morning. Everybody's home on Sunday morning. Where the hell were you?"

She murmured, "I was out walking, I guess." Her anger was checked for a moment. She had imagined it so clearly—Paul leaving the boxes at her door and slipping away. She could not imagine him waiting in front of the house, waiting and watching for her. She felt a chill. She said, "Have you been calling me, too? Letting the phone ring once, then hanging up?"

"Christ. You make it sound like I'm playing some stupid prank." He hesitated, then went on. "Okay. A couple of times I started to call. Then I'd remember that time—just after it happened—when I called and you hung up on me. I mean, I used to sit there while some guy was trying to sell you magazine subscriptions or some damned thing, and you'd listen to him for half an hour. And you hung up on *me*."

"I didn't think we had anything more to say to each other. I don't know what you want from me now."

"Look, it was a rotten thing that happened to you. I concede that. But by now you must understand that it wasn't my fault. There was nothing I could do about it."

"I don't know. I don't think about it anymore."

"I don't think about it anymore," he repeated primly, sarcastically. "That means you've got it all settled? I'm not perfect, I'm not all-powerful, so you've written me off. Good God, Megan, I'd have forgiven you *any*thing by now."

"So that's what you're after. Forgiveness. I didn't pick that up. When people want to be forgiven they usually say they're sorry."

But Paul wasn't listening any more. He braked abruptly,

causing Megan to lurch forward in her seat. He turned in a driveway and started back the way they had come, driving slowly now. Her corner came up at last, and he pulled the wheel around as if he were hauling up something heavy at the end of a rope. "I can't believe this," he said. "All the time I was making up my mind to come to see you, all the time I was waiting in the car, I kept telling myself, this is the toughest part right here. Once you're back with her everything will be all right. You'll wonder why it took you so long. Now it's turned out worse than I ever dreamed it could."

So he had come to this at last. It had always worked for him. He had only to let her know that he was unhappy, and she would do anything, for there was no more potent force in the world for her than Paul Wyler's dissatisfaction. Even now she could feel the urge to yield and comfort, like a tug on a hook embedded deep inside her. But she kept silent.

The car came to a stop in front of her building. She leaned forward, reaching for the door handle. Paul put out a hand to stop her. "Look. I started out on the wrong note tonight. Let me try again, all right?"

Megan sighed. This was so dreary and inevitable. She should have known that he was too much the lawyer to let her go without chiseling some concession from her. She shook her head, not looking at him. "No. There's no point."

"Well, I happen to think there is."

"I mean that I won't be here much longer." She was surprised to hear herself say this; she had not planned to. "I've decided to move away from here."

"Why?"

"I'm tired of New York metro. I'd like to live someplace where you don't get honked at for not running a yellow light."

"But where would you go?"

"West."

There was a moment's pause, and then Paul said, "Well, now, from Stamford, Connecticut, that covers a lot of ground. You mean west like White Plains, or west like San Francisco?"

"Somewhere in between, I guess."

"You're not serious about this. You're just saying it to put me off."

"No. I've been thinking about it for a long time."

"But I thought you were looking for a job around here. Isn't that what you told Heather?"

Megan had the sensation of missing a step in darkness, of coming down unexpectedly and heavily upon a twisting foot. "Oh—when I came by the firm," she mumbled. "You heard about that."

He had not noticed the change in her. He was dejectedly running a finger around the rim of the steering wheel. "Yeah. In the worst possible way, of course. I assumed you'd just picked up another para job. When I heard you were working a typing job at one of those awful places on the wrong side of the tracks, that's what did it. I had to come see you."

Megan sat wondering at her blindness. She had known that her visit would be the talk of the office—why hadn't she foreseen that it would come to Paul's ears, that it might bring him to see her? A vague, pervasive fear spread through her, that she had lost some crucial sense of how the world worked, how people behaved.

Paul was drumming his fingers on the wheel. "So how come you changed your mind so fast? Saturday you're looking for a job around here, Monday you're striking out for God knows where."

"I didn't change my mind. I never told Heather I was looking for a para job *here*. I'll look for one—wherever I get to. Because I'm leaving, that's why I had to copy the papers now."

She stopped speaking, and in the silence her laborious and flimsy fabrication seemed to blow away like a scrap of paper. The lie was a plausible one, but that did not matter. He did not believe it. She knew that, she could feel his bewilderment give way to suspicion. It was as palpable as a drop in temperature or a dimming of light. Lying to Paul was not like lying to other people.

He said, "What did you take?"

"What?"

"I was just wondering what sort of thing a probate para uses for a work sample. I know what a litigation person would use, but you can't very well show people a column of figures or a tax return, can you?"

Megan's mind went blank. A silence fell like water closing over her head. She tried to think, but the awareness of moments passing filled her mind so that nothing else could get in. Every second that went by made it worse, made more obvious the fact that she was lying. But Paul only waited.

"There was a receipt and release," she said at last, much, much too late. "And that trust agreement for the Harmons, the one Jim let me draft myself. And then there was that research memo I did for you. On filing procedures in Middlesex County."

"Oh, yeah. In the Greenberg matter. I thought I closed that file, though. Sent it to storage."

"I wouldn't know. I got the copy from the research file in the library." She had come up with the lie more quickly this time.

"Uh-huh. What else?"

She almost began to think of an answer, almost yielded to the rhythm of the interrogation. But interrogation was Paul's business. He would keep on jabbing at her with these short, toneless questions until she was backed into a corner and stumbling over her own answers.

"No," she said. "That's all."

"So you've got only three work samples? That won't be very impressive."

She got out of the car and slammed the door behind her. She was halfway to the front door when she heard the thin whine of the power window.

"Megan."

She turned.

"I don't get it. Are you doing this just because you enjoy trying to make a fool of me, or is there some particular reason?"

He stared at her, and his cold anger reached into the depths of her heart. When it was clear that she had no answer, he turned away. The window glided up and he drove off into the night.

6

At eight the next morning she was waiting in her car at Old Greenwich train station—the station before Stamford, just as Steve had demanded. But he was not on the first train, or the second. As the third went clattering on its way, and the passengers dispersed hurriedly from the windswept platform, she was afraid that he wasn't coming at all.

She did not recognize him until he was only a few steps from the car. He was dressed strangely, his blond hair covered by a felt hat with a sagging brim, his body enveloped in a long, shabby dress overcoat. Then she realized that he had deliberately altered his appearance for this visit to Stamford. The simple disguise was effective: he was completely changed. He looked drab and timid.

"Okay, let's go," he ordered, even before he had the door closed behind him.

"Wait. Something's happened. We've got to talk first."

"We talk on the way. I don't like sitting in the car with you when we got these people walking by. Understand?"

She started the car and drove off. Steve did not give her a chance to speak before going on. "When we get there, for Christ's sake don't rush right up in front of the house and then stamp on your brakes. That's the kind of thing makes people notice. Soon as you turn on the street, you drive along slow—

not *crawling*, just slow, and you keep it nice and steady all the way down the street. Just keep going. I'll tell you if I want another pass. And maybe I will. I'm going to take a good look at this place, and if I don't like what I see, Ray and you can find yourselves somebody else. 'Cause for me there's plenty of easy scores around. I don't need this."

Out of the corner of her eye, she could see him looking out at the passing scenery of Old Greenwich, the prim houses, the hedges and trees, the winding lanes where there were no cars parked along the curb and no pedestrians. It was enemy country to him: he was rattled. That would make him more likely to listen to her, and she took heart. She said, "That's what I'm trying to tell you, Steve. Something's happened. It can't be tomorrow night. We have to put it off."

"Put it off? Till when? I thought you said Thanksgiving was the only time it would work."

"Yes. I mean—I did say that. I don't know till when, but we can't go tomorrow night. I'm afraid somebody's on to us."

"What are you talking about?"

"The Elkins' lawyer, my old boss—he came to see me last night."

"What for?"

"Just to—to see how I was. But that doesn't matter. What matters is . . . remember, I had to go back to the office for the papers? Somebody saw me."

"Shit. You tell Klausner about that?"

"No. That part was okay. I had an explanation for being there, and she believed me. But my old boss heard I'd been there."

"He wanted to know what you were doing with the old lady's papers? *Shit*. What'd you tell him?"

"No. He doesn't know I have the papers."

He raised his hands. "You lost me, lady. If he doesn't know about the papers—"

"He could tell that I was keeping something back." In frustration she burst out: "He's Mrs. Elkin's lawyer. He knows what happened to me. He knows—he knows me. As soon as he hears about the robbery he'll put it all together. He'll know I had something to do with it."

He was looking over at her. After a long moment he said, "Okay. Pull over."

A restaurant was coming up on her right. It hadn't opened yet and the parking lot was empty. She pulled in behind the building and stopped the car. Steve swept the absurd hat off his head and his forelock fell forward. It was the first time she had seen him in daylight. The bright sunshine caught in his blond eyelashes, softened the flat blue eyes. He looked very young. "This is a bitch," he said. "Maybe you better fill me in on what happened. The whole story."

Megan shook her head.

"Ray just said you got canned 'cause of this old lady. You better explain the whole thing to me. I mean, you say this lawyer guy is going to catch on 'cause of what happened. You better tell me what happened."

"I can't explain. It's all about office politics and tax law. It's too complicated. I can't explain."

Steve grinned. "What—'cause I'm too dumb?"

"I didn't mean—"

" 'Cause I already figured out that you and this guy had a thing going. If that's what you don't want to tell me."

Megan bowed her head and shut her eyes tight.

"I been fired from a few jobs, but my boss never came around later to see how I was doing. Okay? So let's hear it. You were in tight with the boss like that, you must've made some big mistake to get fired."

He was getting out his cigarettes, sliding his shoulders around, making himself comfortable to hear the story. Megan told him. It took a long time. He kept asking her questions, then trying to beat her to the answers. It made her think of her school days, of the bright boy in class who would raise his hand until he was standing up, whining the teacher's name in his eagerness to demonstrate how clever he was. She could not think why Steve wanted to know all this. Perhaps he was getting even with her for that moment of reluctance, of what he thought was condescension. By the time she finished she felt emptied out.

Steve sat silent, smoking. By now the gray film filled the car. She turned her head away and opened the window.

"Okay. Screw this drive-by. You're taking me back to the station."

She turned back in surprise, not daring to believe that it could be this easy. "Then you agree? You see it has to be put off?"

"Well, I got to talk to Klausner. The big boss man. But me, I'm with you. I mean, you say this guy is gonna suspect, is gonna take it to the cops. And you ought to know. When you're crazy about somebody, they can fool you. But when it's all over, you know 'em real well. So this deal doesn't look so great to me no more. Take me back to the station."

He didn't speak on the drive back, but only sat looking out the window. She wondered if his thoughts were already on those other scores, the ones that would be so easy. She hoped so.

That evening, when she came home from work, he was waiting for her. She did not turn at the first beep of the car horn, and at the second, when she did turn and saw him beckoning her from behind the wheel, she stood and stared for a moment before she went over and got in.

"What's the matter? You forget all about me?" His voice sounded different, quick and husky. She could see his teeth in the darkness of the car. He was grinning.

"It's the car," she said. The car was a small yellow import—not at all the sort of car she would have expected Steve to drive. "I suppose you're back because—I suppose you're not going to put it off?"

"You got it. I mean, it's put back, but only by twenty-four hours. I go in Thanksgiving night."

"One *day?*" Her voice sounded like a wail. "What difference will that make? Why?"

"It's Klausner's idea. I'm not too crazy about it either." He chuckled. "Hey, if sitting around another day bugs you, just think what it would be like if we put the job off weeks or months. Sitting around, waiting—you wouldn't want that, huh?"

Megan sat silent. She did not know what she wanted any more, but she knew what she had expected—that she would not see Steve again, that her sight of him striding back to the train station that morning would be the last. Having hit a snag, busy, cheery Ray Klausner would move on to something else, and forget about her. There would be no robbery. With the routines of her work, a dull calmness had come over her. The robbery became like a vivid dream, fading slowly now that she was awake. But suddenly she was plunged into it again.

"I should've known. That Klausner, you give him a chance and he complicates things for you. He's been making calls to his clients, and he found out he couldn't do much business Thanksgiving Day. So, he doesn't want the stuff sitting around his shop. So, the job's moved to Thanksgiving night. The day after Thanksgiving, that's a heavy shopping day," Steve said, and laughed.

Megan flinched, gripping the door handle reflexively. "I can't drive you by the house now. It's too late to see anything. It's too late."

"No problem. I already cased it out. Bought a map, went by on my own. Looks great, terrific. No problem."

He put his arms over his head and stretched. He looked confined in the small car, as if it would burst with his restlessness and eagerness. Ray Klausner must have done a selling job on him, to have changed his mood so much from what it had been that morning. Or perhaps it was cruder than that. Perhaps Klausner had given him drugs. She remembered being with people at college who were on speed or cocaine, and they had been like this, moving so fast that you could not get through to them.

She recognized a cold certainty that had been at the back of her mind all along: her part in this business had been played out. Even if she wanted to, she could not stop these men now. She said listlessly, "By the time I'm in danger, by the time the police come after me, you'll be long gone. It doesn't matter to you."

"Aw, come on, lady. Lay off that kind of talk. Me and Ray talked it over, and you got no problem, far as we can see."

"Paul will know. He'll go to the police."

"Yeah. So what?"

She stared at him in surprise.

"So he tells the cops, this girl used to work for me, I think she could maybe've been in on the job. That don't give the cops nothing they can use on you. All they can do is put you on their list of suspects. And lady, that's going to be a long list. Anybody knew the place was going to be empty Thanksgiving could've tipped the job. The paperboy. The guy that delivers groceries. The maid. The maid's got to be a nigger or a spick, right? Prob'ly lives in some project that's crawling with nigger or spick crooks. The cops are going to be much more interested in somebody like that. With you, they'll be thinking, how could somebody like her ever meet up with a fence or a B and E guy? It was just a lucky break you walked into Klausner's place. Nobody knows about that. You don't even have to make up some story for the cops, 'cause they're not going to know what questions to ask."

After the long rush of excited speech, he lapsed reluctantly into silence. Megan became conscious of a remote pain. She let go of the door handle. She had been gripping it so tightly that there was a red imprint on her palm, visible even in the faint streetlight. She said: "The police are going to interrogate me."

"It won't be so tough. You got no record. You got a fixed address and a job. You're a straight citizen. They won't pull any shit on you."

"I don't think I can stand . . ."

"Being called into the station? It's not so bad."

"No, I don't think I can stand . . ."

"Stand what?"

"Paul knowing." The words just came out, spoken with the thought. She listened to them as if someone else had said them, not knowing what they meant, yet knowing they were important.

Steve laughed. He laughed so loudly and unexpectedly that she jumped. "Don't you get it? Him knowing makes it better."

"Makes it better?"

"Yeah. It's all like a big joke on him. He'll know what you pulled, only he can't do *shit* about it. Don't you get it? You just got to stay cool, be smart, after the job. Like nothing's changed. You keep plugging away at your shit job and living in your same lousy place and wearing your same lousy clothes." He paused and straightened up away from her. He had been leaning close, chuckling as he spoke, so that she had felt the rush of hot breath and the spray of spittle on her cheek. "Then, after a while, the cops lose interest in you, and you get the money from wherever you put it away, and you take off. Start new someplace else, like we talked about before. Remember?"

Megan said nothing. She remembered, though, when Steve had first said those words, and they had given her such a surge of hope. She had built so much upon them; she had built a future that was clear and bright and beckoning, as if she were standing on a street, looking in a beautiful shop window. But now the curtains had been drawn.

Steve was twisting the key, starting the motor. There was nothing more to say. Megan opened the door and started to get out. "See you at Klausner's Friday morning," he said, and this seemed to amuse him too. She shut the door on his laughter. The car pulled noisily away.

Megan went for a walk on Thanksgiving Day. For once she did not have the suburban sidewalks to herself, because the weather was overcast but mild, and it was the hour when people arose from the table to walk off their feasts. She passed several family groups, the adults moving in stately, surfeited procession while the children dashed around and shouted in front of them.

She came to a seaside park. There were many strollers here, too, squishing over the wet ground and thin grass. She had to make her way around a couple of muddy and uproarious touch football games. She noticed that she was the only person who was alone. Not that it mattered, but she took note of anything about herself that might make people remark or remember her.

She walked on until she came to the beach. Down here the wind was raw, and there was no one else around. Seagulls yelped and cawed. The tide was low. The sea, looking as dingy as used bathwater, was running out and leaving a ring of debris behind on the slick gray sand: straggling seaweed and kelp, garbage, broken shells and parts of crab's bodies. She looked across the bay, at the eastern flank of Shippan Point, with its big houses and dense bare trees. You could not see the Elkin house from here, it was too far inland.

She had gone there, though, yesterday. They had been let off work in midafternoon, and when she reached the corner of Shippan Avenue, she had turned and walked down it. Very soon, before she expected it, the corner with the sign that said SHADY LA. came up. She paused and lifted her head and looked.

The street had changed almost beyond recognition in the six weeks since she had seen it. It belied its name now; there was no shade, but only the long crooked shadows of the bare trees, striping the street and the dun-colored lawns. The houses, no longer embowered in greenery, stood out like goods on a shelf. She could even see the Elkin house—its gray-shingled bulk and gabled roof loomed over its smaller neighbor. There was only one car in the drive, a long blue limousine. She could descry the orange dot of the New York license plate. The car had been sent by the uncle, then, or rented. Its trunk stood open; somebody might come out of the house any moment. Megan turned away.

She did not go home, though. She walked all the way down Shippan Avenue, to the place where it ended at the edge of the sea, then turned and came slowly back. The limousine was gone by then, the house dark, but for a single light left burning in a front window, like a beacon announcing that the house was empty. For a moment she was angry at Mrs. Elkin for her insouciance. Thinking about it now, she realized how absurd that had been. But she did not smile.

She left the bleak beach and walked back through the park. Night was falling by the time she got home. The sun had gone down invisibly behind the dense overcast.

She sat on the sofa for a long while. She had taken off her

watch and unplugged the clock, so she could tell time only by the noises that came through the walls and floor. In the apartment below, the television snapped off during the concluding roar of a football game. Then she heard the murmur of conversation, mixed with clinking silverware and occasional gusts of laughter, as the family supped on their leftovers. Much later, talk came echoing up the stairwell, cars started up outside, and the guests drove away amid shouted good-byes. Then there was dishwashing: the long, whistling torrent through the pipes. She heard shouts and wails and the stomping of feet overhead, as the little boy upstairs resisted being put to bed.

For a while after that, footsteps or voices came to her faintly from here and there in the building, and then there was silence. Utter silence. The silence of late night. Megan tried to guess the time, then tried to stop herself from doing so. She did not know when Steve would go in, or how long he would take. The tormenting thought crossed her mind that she would still be fretting hours after he was away and it was all over. There was nothing she could do until morning, when it would be time to go to New York. She ached with the longing for sleep, for unconsciousness to blot out the next hours.

But she did not go to bed. She knew that if she undressed, got between the sheets and turned off the light, sleep would flee from her. Instead she made herself a mug of herbal tea and stretched out on the sofa with a blanket and a book. She hoped that sleep, like a wary bird, could be lured by her inattention to it.

So she sipped the weak, cooling tea, and ran her eye over the page again and again until she managed to wring some sense from it.

She did not know that she had fallen asleep until she woke suddenly. She lifted her groggy head and opened her eyes. It was a sound that had awakened her. The tea kettle was whistling. She must have left a low light under it. She was angry at herself for this blunder; she could only have been asleep for a few minutes.

She pulled herself upright, put her feet to the floor. With movement her mind cleared. The shrill sound that had awakened her was not the whistling of a kettle. It was a siren.

PART III

1

The siren wailed on, thin and high in the distance. It pulsed so that she could not tell if it was coming nearer or going away. There was the same confused apprehension she'd felt so many times in her car on the road when she heard a siren—how far away was the police car, which direction was it coming from?—but a thousand times worse.

She took a step, stumbled, untangled the blanket from her legs, and went to the window. There was nothing to see, there was only the traffic light flashing yellow at the end of her street. Her groggy mind fenced with the fear. This had nothing to do with her—it couldn't. No need to think that. Maybe it wasn't even a police car at all, but an ambulance or a fire truck. She had been acutely conscious of sirens during the last few days, and when you were listening for them you heard them all the time. All the time.

The vehicle was coming nearer. The pulsing wail mounted and diminished less each time. Shrillness filled up the fragile bowl of her ear with pain and she could not hear anymore. The car shot through the intersection in a shower of lights. It was a police car, it was going toward Shippan Point, toward Shady Lane. Gradually the noise diminished, and she was able to hear the other sirens.

The night was full of sirens. They whooped and howled, the noise seeming to catch and spread in senseless imitation, like the barking of dogs. Megan turned away from the window and sat down on the edge of the sofa. There was nothing she could do. There were too many.

Too many. She grasped at the thought. Even if the worst had happened, even if they had caught Steve, they would not need so many cars. There must be a fire, or a big pile-up on the turnpike. It had to be something much worse than a burglary, something unconnected with her.

She hunched over on the sofa, her hands clenched and gripped tightly between her thighs, rocking slightly like a distressed and helpless child. At last the sirens began to die down. In the end there was just a far-off shimmer of sound, fading away. Still, it was what she listened to, and the other, nearer sound must have been going on for a long time before she heard it.

It was a light, insistent tapping. It came from the back door. She got up and ran into the kitchen, switching on the light. She couldn't see anything through the glass in the door but the tapping went on. She scrabbled at the chain and pulled the door open.

Steve pitched into the room, almost knocking her down. He had been crouched down against the door.

"Get that light off!"

He hardly got the hoarse whisper out. His breathing was a ragged wheeze. Megan reached a hand out with what seemed unendurable slowness and swept it over the switch. The room went dark. Steve moved; she saw him for a moment in the lighted doorway, and then he put out the lamp in there.

She followed. He was kneeling at the front window, looking down into the street. Spokes of light raked the ceiling. Megan went to crouch beside him.

The police car was creeping along the street, its rooflight rippling, the siren mute. A spotlight played along the cars parked at the curb. It drew nearer. As it passed beneath the window she could see the watch on the wrist of the man who was operating the spotlight. Finally it passed from their sight, and there was a roar of the engine as it accelerated away.

Steve twisted and collapsed, leaning his back against the wall, and the sound of his rasping breath again filled the room. Megan realized she had stopped breathing too. Her knees were quivering and she sank down on the sofa.

"What happened?" she whispered. "What went wrong?"

Even in the darkness she could see that Steve's whole body was arching and buckling with the effort to draw in air. Fear had driven him to run beyond the point of collapse. For a long time he could not answer.

"Had to leave the van," he said at last. "They got the end of the street blocked off in front of me. Ran the other way. Got to this fence and went over it. Then I was on a beach, a goddam beach. Nothing in front of me but water. Cops coming up behind. I went along the shore. There was loose rocks. I kept stumbling. Kept ending up in water up to my knees. I could hear the cars. Didn't think I'd make it. Didn't think I'd make it." He broke off, coughing, and had to wait and breathe for a moment. "Then I came up against somebody's back wall. Not too high, went over it. Ran through the yard, through a bunch of yards. Had to stay off the street. There was dogs barking, lights coming on. I went through a driveway, came out on that main road. And there was nothing there, man. No people, no cars. There was nobody out there except me and the cops. Couldn't stay out on the streets, couldn't get out of this fucking town without a car. Had to come here."

Now he turned to look at her. She could not see his face, but only the movement of his head. She said: "I don't hear the sirens any more. I guess it's all right."

Steve gasped and coughed again. He struggled to his feet and went past her, into the bathroom. She heard the sound of dry retching. It went on and on. When it stopped there was silence. He did not come back.

She got up and took a hesitant step toward the bathroom, then another. The light wasn't on, and Steve was only a huddled shadow. He was sitting on the floor, his knees drawn up, his head bowed and hidden deep in his folded arms. He made no noise at all, but he was shaking.

Then abruptly he jerked his head up. Megan backed away. It was instinctive, as if she had come upon a wounded animal which would snap at her if she got too close.

Steve rose and opened the medicine cabinet. His hand pawed at the shelves and things went clattering into the sink. "You got anything?"

"What do you need?"

"Pills. You got any pills for Christ's sake. I'm real wired. I got to come down. You got any—whatchacallit—Valium, anything like that."

She shook her head.

He brushed past her and returned to the kitchen. The light went on. Megan stood still. She tried to make her mind bear down, grasp what was happening. It was all for nothing, she thought. There'll be no money now. All for nothing. But that was only a small, muttering voice and her head was like a roomful of shouting voices, and she could make no sense of any of them.

In the kitchen Steve had found the bottle of whiskey. His gloved hand fumbled at the cap until he got it off. Then he upended the bottle and drank as much of the astringent liquor as he could at a gulp. Then he tipped the bottle again. In the light she could see that his jeans and sneakers were soaked and muddy. There were big stains mottling the dark sheen of his windbreaker, and tiny spots like freckles all over his face. As he raised the bottle again she flinched a little, because between his glove and cuff his hairy wrist was caked with red-brown blood.

"You're hurt."

Steve looked at the wrist so close to his eyes, then turned away, set the bottle down hard, bent his whole body protectively over his injury.

"Oh, Christ, I don't know how I got into this . . ." He stared over his shoulder at her. "You. You told me the place would be empty. You guaranteed it."

Megan knew than that it was not just the wrist—the speckles on his face were blood, and the huge stains on his jacket were blood. But it was not he who was injured. "What happened? Oh God, what happened?" Her voice sounded soft, distant.

"I wasn't expecting nothing. I'd been in there a long time, things were fine. I was in the upstairs hall. Cutting a picture out of the frame. And then all of a sudden there's lights going on, alarms—no, it wasn't alarms, musta been her yelling. I didn't know what was going on. Didn't know who it was. Couldn't see anything except there was somebody between me and the door and I had to get out of there."

"Is she dead? Oh my God—is she dead?"

"How the fuck do I know? I just wanted out." Then there was a ripple in his cheek as his jaw set. "No use kidding ourselves. She's dead. I had the knife right there and I cut her."

The blow was too great. Megan could neither feel nor think. One long moment of her life was seared blank. When she came to herself again, she heard Steve talking. After a time the sense of the words began to get through to her. He was talking again about his flight from the police, about the darkness and his desperation. Megan thought: My God, he thinks all this is something that's happening to *him.*

She had to get away from him, get out of the light. She fled into the darkness of the next room. She almost had the front door open when Steve caught up with her. They grappled. She was clumsy, softened by shock, and he was merely fending off her hands from the doorknob. Their movements were as slow as if they were underwater, and Megan kept reaching for the door instinctively, as if it were the surface of the water. She would drown if she couldn't break through it.

But he got a grip on each of her wrists and pushed her backward until she stumbled and fell to the couch. Still she struggled against him, tried to get to her feet.

"What're you trying to do?" he whispered hoarsely. "Go out in the street? There's cops all over—or maybe that's it, huh? You're gonna flag down a cop car, you're gonna yell for *help?*"

His breath, hot and stinking of whiskey, rushed into her face. In the words she recognized what she was going to do. "You can't stop me," she said. "I don't care what you do." She kept on struggling to free her wrists, to get to her feet.

"I'm not going to do nothing to you. You got hold of the wrong idea. There's no help for you out there. You and me got to help each other."

The softness of his tone disturbed her. "I'm not helping you. This is the end. I never meant for anybody to get hurt."

"You think I did? I just panicked. 'Cause you told me the place was gonna be empty."

"It should have been empty. It had to be. I never meant for anybody to get hurt. It was a—a—"

"A mistake?" he supplied for her. "Sure. You made a mistake. Only you know what the law calls it? Felony murder. Ever heard of that—felony murder?"

He had let go of her wrists now. She had not realized when it happened. She made no effort to get up. She was listening to him now.

"Listen good 'cause I know all about this. When you're in the bucket guys got nothing to talk about but what the DA's charging 'em with, what their lawyer's trying to get it knocked down to. Felony murder law says that when somebody gets killed in a job, everybody who was in on the job is in on the killing. That's it. You got excuses, they don't give a shit. Doesn't matter if you didn't do it. Doesn't matter if you weren't there. You were in on the job, they charge you with first-degree murder. Premeditated murder. Shit, I didn't premeditate nothing. I didn't know what was going on. But they'll hit me for premeditated murder. Same thing for you."

Megan heard her voice murmuring weakly. "She couldn't have been there. I saw the car. And then the car was gone. She couldn't—"

"She was there. She's dead."

Megan put up her hands as if they would keep the words away from her. She could not stand any more words. But Steve was through talking. She could sense him waiting. After a long time she said, "What do I have to do?"

"Nothing. Not a thing. When the sun comes up, when there's cars on the street, you drive me out of here. But for now you wait. I'm gonna get cleaned up."

"No!" She whispered urgently. "The pipes—the water in the pipes is too loud. The neighbors will hear—if they haven't already—"

110

"Take it easy. They ain't heard nothing. We been talking soft this whole time. I got soft shoes on, you're in your socks. They heard nothing. You're right about the pipes, though. I'll wait." His husky whisper was soothing, amenable. They had an understanding now, she and Steve.

"Tolls coming up." Steve shifted in his seat to dig in his pocket.

But despite the warning, when she rounded the curve and saw that her way was barred, saw the flashing lights and the uniformed men, Megan's mind and body seized up with fear. The car drifted toward the side of the road, like a boat caught in a current.

Steve's hand gripped the wheel, set them back on course. His voice close to her ear ordered, "Slow up. Easy now." When they were in the bay and stopped he took her hand and turned it over, pressed the cold discs of change into it. "Roll down the window, throw the money in the chute. Okay, light's green, you can go. Easy, huh? We're halfway there." He sat back in his seat, grinning, and lit a cigarette.

They drove on in silence. Tall, jagged buildings loomed up on the horizon, then closed in on the roadway, pressing in upon it from both sides. The road dipped and veered. It squeezed between high embankments, burrowed through black tunnels. Steve had begun to recover his spirits the moment they crossed the state line, and now that they were in the city he was himself again. His face and hands were clean, and his stained jacket was balled up in his lap. He fiddled with the radio until he found a station he liked, then moved his body to the music. He shouted abuse at other drivers who got in their way. His restless energy seemed to fill the car, to crowd Megan against the door, until the handle jabbed her ribs. She retreated deep into her thoughts.

How could it have happened? She had seen the car on Wednesday afternoon, and then the car was gone. The car with New York plates, the uncle's car sent to fetch them. She had seen the light left on in the empty house. Mrs. Elkin could not have been there last night. Megan worked it all out, as if she had not been through it all before while she sat on the couch in the dark, waiting for the dawn. As if she could prove, like a theorem in geometry, that Mrs. Elkin could not have been there. As if she could reason Mrs. Elkin back to life.

"I don't understand. I don't know what she was doing there."

The sound of her voice startled her; she had not meant to speak. Steve was irritated. He got his cigarettes out but he had gone through the pack, and he crumpled it up and threw it out the window.

"If she was home, she wouldn't have been by herself. It doesn't make sense."

He switched the radio off with a sharp twist of the dial. "Leave it alone, for Christ's sake. It happened. Forget about it."

Megan gave a gasp of incredulity and pain. "Forget about it?"

"That's what I said. Okay, you feel bad about the lady getting killed. You think you're going to feel any better if you get caught?"

She turned to glance at him.

"Don't give me that look like I'm a piece of shit. Just think about what I'm saying, 'cause you got a choice to make. You want to get caught? Want to be stuck in a room with them asking you questions over and over? They get you to answer and that's not the end. They'll make you go over it again and again. They write it up and make you sign. Then they get you in court and you got to listen to it all over again, mixed up with a lot of lies and bullshit. And then the judge says you got to be locked up. When you're in prison, you think you're going to feel any better?"

Megan had to slow down. A car honked and swept past. All that he described was very clear in her mind, and she felt sick. She said, "No."

"You made your choice then." He shifted in his seat. "Bridge toll coming up. Don't go nuts on me again, okay?"

There was a line of cars this time and they had to wait. When they were through the gates, she stepped on the accelerator and broke free of traffic, soared out onto the high bridge. The sun was clear of the horizon now. The water lay glittering and blue beneath the wide, clear sky. It was a blustery day— she could feel the winds against the car. She said, "I could keep on driving."

"Yeah. You could. Course, when they find out you ran, they'll know to come after you. You better get away far and fast. Only you can't hang on to this car too long. Better not use any credit cards, show any ID . . ." He looked over at her. 'You're not really going to run for it."

Megan nodded, knowing it was true. She had merely stumbled upon a piece of wreckage that was still in her mind, a remnant of her hopes: the drive west. The new life.

"Your office open today?"

The question threw her for a moment. She nodded.

"Then you better show up for work. Beat it back there. You don't want to do anything that will make people ask you questions. Thing for you to do is stick it out. Just like we talked about before."

"Everything's different now."

"No. Her being dead, that makes it worse if you get caught. Doesn't make it any easier for them to catch you. It's just like we talked about."

Megan said, "Paul is the executor. He's one of the first they'll notify. He knows by now. Maybe he's told the police by now."

"Uh-uh. A guy'll hand you up for burglary, he won't when it's murder. When somebody gets killed people don't want to get mixed up in it. They keep their mouths shut. At least, till the cops really lean on them."

They had left the bridge behind now. After a few miles he pointed to a graffiti-covered road sign. "This is it. You get off here."

It was unexpected. She veered sharply over to the off-ramp. "But I thought—"

"You thought what?"

"Nothing."

"You thought we were going to Ray's?" He laughed again. "What for? We got nothing for him. He's prob'ly heard what happened, and made up his mind he don't know us. Klaus-ner's a real busy man. He's got no time for fuck-ups. Listen to me, lady, and don't go near the guy. 'Cause this time you're not going to get the easy chair and the cup of coffee."

Megan nodded. That was just something else that had stuck in her mind—the drive to Ray's to get her money, the drive she had meant to be making at this moment. She was behind. She had not caught up with what had happened. Even now.

At the bottom of the ramp he told her to turn left. After a moment he said, "Okay, this is close enough." She pulled over to the curb and Steve opened the door. She had been longing to be rid of him, but now she did not want him to leave her alone. She said, "What will you do?"

He paused with one foot on the curb. "Do? You mean am I going to run? Hide? What for? I'm okay. Sure they got the van, but that won't do 'em any good. I stole the van off the street. I had gloves on the whole time I was in it. Won't do 'em any good. Had to leave my tools, but they're clean. No marks, no numbers, no prints. I'm always real careful in case I have to leave 'em. *I* didn't make no mistakes on this job."

He got out and slammed the door so hard that the car shook. Megan turned around, through the uprights of the elevated tracks that crossed the intersection. As she drove past, Steve was going around the corner, striding along with his jacket under his arm, as if it were summer and he were out for a stroll.

2

The signal was red as she came down the ramp from the turnpike in Stamford. She stopped the car and sat staring at the light. She was not going to be able to do this. She could not go to the office and sit at her desk and wait for the police to come. It was impossible. When the signal changed she did not turn right, toward the plant. She turned left and drove under the turnpike, then turned again and pulled into the garage entrance of Goldman Lasch's office building. The guard raised the bar out of her way without leaving his booth. The parking sticker was still on her windshield. She drove over to the stairway, where she knew there was a pay phone.

With the receiver in one hand and the coin in the other she made herself hold still, made herself wait for second thoughts to catch up with her. But there were none. He'd hand you up for the burglary, Steve had said, but not when it's murder. When somebody gets killed people don't want to get mixed up in it. She had not really registered his words when he said them, but on the drive back she had recalled them and thought about them until her mind was racked with pain. She had to see Paul, she had to know what he would do. She dropped in the coin and dialed.

It rang for a long time. When the office was closed—as it was today—and there was no one at the switchboard, the telephone bell would jangle down the corridors until somebody, if there was anybody at all, picked it up. Paul ought to be there. He would have been awakened hours ago, and he would be at the office, unless he was with the family, or the police.

"Goldman Lasch. Paul Wyler speaking."

She was conscious of drawing in her breath. "Paul, it's me."

He was silent. She felt as if she were sending her words spinning into a void. "You've got to come talk to me."

"Where are you?"

"In the building. The . . . uh . . . the third parking level."

"I'll come down."

Megan put the receiver back. The parking levels were open-sided and the cold wind off the sound rushed in. She had no coat. She hunched her shoulders and folded her arms over her breast. Unable to stay still, she began to pace.

If he was willing to talk to her at all, he could not be sure of what she had done. He could not have gone to the police yet. Surely that was true. Wasn't it? Megan was unable to think clearly any more. She knew only that she would say anything to stop him from going to the police.

Apart from the wind and the buzzing of the lights it was quiet in the nearly empty garage. She heard Paul's footsteps echoing through the concrete vault a moment before he appeared. The wind peeled his suitcoat away from his vest and blew his hair back from his forehead. He had his glasses on. His face, when he came close enough for her to see it, told her nothing. But then Paul had the lawyer's art of making his face a mask.

He took her elbow and led her through the door to the stair landing. They were out of the wind now, but she stayed hunched over, her arms wrapped around herself. Paul let go of her elbow and moved away, to lean against the opposite wall. He put his hands in his pockets. The relaxed stance was a pose. He was rigid with tension. His eyes behind the glasses were fixed on her, but he said nothing. It was as if he were wary of her.

"I heard what happened. I heard it on the radio." Her voice had a faint echo in the stairwell.

"Yes. I thought that was why you'd come."

"Well of course I had to come here. I know how this is going to look. As if I had something to do with it."

"It was a professional burglar." Paul's voice was low and taut. "They found his tools, so they know that. They're looking around for somebody who could have tipped him off to the Elkins, because that's the way professionals work."

Megan backed away from him. She pressed herself against the door. "You've talked to them already. To the police."

"No. It was somebody I know in the state attorney's office. Her name's Stephanie Feltch. She called at six this morning to notify me."

"To notify you."

He shifted his shoulders against the wall and frowned. "She asked me some questions. She wanted to know who did the inventory. The appraisals. Who in the office handled the file. She—"

"You told her about me."

He hesitated. For the first time he looked away from her. "Yes."

Megan held herself in with her arms and hung her head. But her eyes were dry and she was still able to breathe. She did not feel any more afraid. Perhaps that was impossible. Perhaps there was nothing beyond this state of hushed dread.

"I had to tell her you got fired. Had to. There was no other way." His voice was getting shaky now. "Too many people know about that. If she didn't get it from me, she'd get it from somebody else. And I had to tell her about you coming to the firm on Saturday, for the same reason. She'd only get it from somebody else."

"Yes," Megan murmured. "You have to cover your ass, don't you? That's something you told me one time."

Paul did not answer. Instead he said, "The part I changed was Monday night, the night I came to see you."

She lifted her head to look at him. "The part you changed," she said. "The part you *changed?*"

"We didn't argue. You didn't say you were leaving town. I never came to see you at all. Have you got that? Our stories have to agree."

"Why—why did you change—"

"That part about you leaving town, that would have looked really bad. I couldn't let them have that."

"But why—"

"Because I got mad. I was still half-asleep, still in shock from the news, and goddam Stephanie Feltch is pumping me for information." Before her eyes his face had grown flushed and adamant. He straightened up. "I hate the way prosecutors operate. I did when I was with Legal Aid, and I still do. They dump on people who have enough problems already. It's an instinct with them. I mean, it's bad enough, it's rotten enough, that you got fired. And because of that I'm supposed to point the finger at you in a criminal investigation. No way. No *way.*"

He was trembling and his voice rang from the concrete walls. The mask had dropped now, and Megan saw that he was afraid. Of course he was afraid: he had lied to the authorities for her. He had committed a crime, and he would know the wording of the charge, and the length of the prison sentence. But even now she could not tell if he knew what she had done. She said, "It looks bad for me. It must look bad, even to you."

"Megan, is it possible—is it possible that you said something about the Elkins and it got to the wrong ears? I mean—

117

you must have told a lot of people about what happened to you, about the whole mess. That's only natural. When you've been wronged, when you feel outraged, you complain to people about it."

"You think I have lots of people to talk to?" Megan murmured, but he did not hear.

"Do you think it's at all possible that what you said might have gotten to the wrong person? It wouldn't have to be much. Just that there are these rich people, the Elkins, on Shady Lane, and that they're usually away on Thanksgiving."

Megan flinched as if she had been struck upon an old wound. "Why was she there, Paul? Why wasn't she in New York? She was supposed to be in New York."

Paul averted his face. He wanted to pretend she had not asked that question. But she had to know.

"They always go to the uncle's at Thanksgiving. Why was she there, Paul?"

"Her plans changed." He was still keeping his head down. "She took the kids down to their uncle's, they watched the parade and had supper as usual. But then she came back on her own. She wanted some quiet time, she told me. She hasn't been well. It's because of the mess with the will, the hearing coming up next week. I told her it was nothing to worry about, but she's—she was a worrier."

Quiet time. That was probably just what she had said. The phrase sounded like Barbara Elkin. Megan could almost hear the voice she had heard six weeks ago. In her mind's eye she glimpsed her—a glimpse that was brief and unclear and searing as a brilliant light. With a sudden jolt Megan saw where she had gone wrong. She was the one who had suffered the most for that mistake in the will, and in her thoughts she had redressed the balance by denying that anyone else suffered for it at all. Her brooding and scheming had flattened out Paul and Barbara Elkin, simplified them. It was easier to hate them that way, easier to manipulate them. But the real people were quite different. They could change their plans. They could worry and be hurt.

She saw it all so clear and whole that for a moment she almost believed that she could do something about it. But she could not. Barbara Elkin was dead.

Something was scraping against her back and she realized that she was sliding down the rough concrete wall, sinking to the floor. She covered her face with her hands, but no tears came. She sensed that Paul was kneeling beside her, and she had something she must say to him. Her lungs ached as she tried to get the breath to speak. "I never thought anyone would get hurt. I didn't mean her any harm."

"I know that. I know that." He took her hands from her face and put his own in their place, gently turned her head until she was looking at him. "It wasn't you. It was the thief. You had nothing to do with that. You just talked to somebody and it got to the wrong people. You're not responsible."

Megan gazed into his face so close to hers, and her old love of him opened his mind to her. He knew this was not true, but he was begging her to go along with it. She owed it to him to lie, to make it easier for him to protect her. But she could not do it.

"No, Paul. What I did, I did on purpose. I took the Elkin inventory from your desk and copied it and gave it to those men. You know that. You must have worked it all out."

His hands slipped away from her face. Kneeling beside her, he bowed his head and let his shoulders sag. For a long moment he did not speak. "Yes," he said at last, "I worked it out. I've been doing a lot of thinking. About what I did, and didn't do. About what you must have gone through, to—"

"I never meant for anyone to get hurt," she said again. "But that doesn't matter, does it? I was their accomplice in the burglary, so I'm guilty of the murder. That's what the law says."

He raised his eyes to hers. "I don't care what the law says."

"But it's true, isn't it? There's a—a felony murder law."

"Yes." His brows drew together in puzzlement. "How did you know? Who told you about that?"

"The thief. They were after him and he had nowhere to run but to me. And to make me help him he told me I was as guilty as he was. He made me drive him back to the city."

"My God." Paul was slowly shaking his head. "How did this guy ever get his hooks into you in the first place? How did he meet you?"

"It wasn't him. It was his boss. A fence. I was in the city

119

selling things, and I happened to go into his shop. And he knew right away what he could do with me."

"You were selling things?"

"Yes. It was that watch you gave me that I sold to him. I—"

Paul put up his hand very suddenly to stop her, but his eyes held hers. "You don't have to explain. You needed money. Of course you'd need money. And you wouldn't want anything around that would remind you of me."

He spoke so simply. Paul's voice for her had always been filled with shadings that she had taught herself to pick up—amusement, irony, irritation. But now there was none of that. He spoke simply and gravely.

"Yes," Megan said, because it was true. "I didn't hate you. But I couldn't stop thinking about you, and I hated my thoughts."

Paul was silent for a long time. Then he said, "I thought about you all the time, but not about what you were going through. Never that. Only about how I was going to get you back. You were making me unhappy, and I was—I was angry at you. That night I came to see you, the things I said—"

"That was Monday night," Megan interrupted. "Monday night never happened."

They exchanged a long look. Then Paul got to his feet and gave her his hand to help her up. "I've got to get back," he said. "There will be people coming into the office and I can't have them wondering where I am."

She nodded. When she had come in here, she had been numb. But now there was warmth and hope in her, and the fear she felt was sharp. "What's going to happen?"

"I don't know. I can't say when you'll be called in, or who will talk to you. But Stephanie will pass on what I told her to the police and to her investigator, and you'll be questioned."

Megan nodded.

"When you get in there don't worry that they'll see you're scared. Anybody's scared when they're sitting in front of one of those microphones and the tape recorder's running, no matter how innocent they are. Just answer the questions. Don't worry about what they think of you. It's all very impersonal, Meg. They just look for a case against you, and if they think there is one, they feed you into the system. It's slow and fumbling, and there are a lot of holes. They won't get you." He had held on to her hand, and he gripped it tightly for a moment and then let it go. "Wait a minute after I'm gone. Just in case there's a car passing. We can't take the chance of being seen together."

"Yes, I understand. But I've got to know when I'll see you again. I won't get through the day without knowing that."

He nodded. "This evening. Around six. I'll call, or I'll come to your place."

Then he was gone.

3

There was only one telephone in the accounting section. It was on Pat the supervisor's desk, at the opposite end of the room from Megan. She could not hear its ring. But something made her glance down the row of desks, over the hunched shoulders of the other women, and she saw Pat looking back at her. Pat raised a large, pale hand and beckoned. She was not smiling. Employees were not supposed to get personal calls.

Megan got up, glancing at the clock: quarter after eleven. Paul's acquaintance Stephanie Feltch had wasted no time in passing on the information about her. She walked up the row to Pat, who was holding the receiver at arm's length.

"Sorry about this."

"Just don't make a practice of it, okay?" Pat turned her back and resumed her typing.

Megan pressed the glowing hold button. She gave her name. It was a woman's voice on the other end: a secretary. She sounded indifferent and harried, as if she had a long list of names to be called and a page of appointments to be juggled. Would Ms. Lofting come in to the state attorney's office to make a statement? Would twelve thirty be convenient? The last question threw Megan for a moment. She had not expected to be given a choice.

Court was not in session on the day after Thanksgiving. The doors stood open upon the dim, empty hearing rooms. The lobby smelled of old cigarette smoke. Megan climbed the stairs and went in the narrow door marked STATE ATTORNEY.

It was an ordinary waiting room, as in a doctor's office, with a row of chairs against the walls and a sliding window through to the reception desk. The plaster underneath was cracked and dirty, as if people had been kicking at it in trapped frustration, the way cattle kicked at their pens. She gave her name, and they told her to wait.

A lot of people were waiting. There were two lean, fidgety Hispanic youths, sitting on either side of their slumped and sad-eyed mother; there was a policeman, sitting awkwardly on one haunch because of his gunbelt and nightstick; there were several lawyers with their briefcases open on their laps, working. Megan thought that she would have to wait a long time, and braced herself for it. But in only a moment the door swung open and a young woman strode up to her, holding out a hand.

"Megan. Thank you for coming. I'm Stephanie Feltch."

She announced herself as if she were used to people being glad to meet her whatever the circumstances, and Megan thought that most men would be. Stephanie Feltch was very good-looking. She was tall and dark, and she had a brilliant smile and a redoubtable jawline. She clasped Megan's hand in her own and held it still, and moved her head fractionally so that her eyes were exactly level with Megan's. They were big, dark eyes, very carefully made up.

"Well, come on in back," she said, as if it were something that Megan was eager to do. She turned and led the way down the narrow corridor. She seemed even taller from the back, and her hips had an easy swing.

The office was small and cluttered; surplus files were stacked beside the cabinet, and there was just room for a narrow metal desk with a chair on either side. Stephanie Feltch sat down, and sighed, and combed both her hands through her luxuriant hair. "First off, I have to apologize. Our investigator was supposed to be here to take your statement, but he's not. Sorry. Can you wait a few minutes?"

"All right," Megan said.

"You do know why you're here?"

"They said on the phone it was about Mrs. Elkin. But I don't know what you expect me to tell you."

Stephanie Feltch gave her another bright, vague smile and made no answer. Instead she went on with her apology. "Ordinarily it would be easy enough to get somebody from the police department to interview you, but they're all down on Shippan Point. Literally. The whole force. The uniforms are looking behind hedges and under cars, in case the perp hid out and fell asleep, and the detectives are doing a neighborhood canvass. Not that anybody can tell them much of anything, but I think the chief and the mayor want the folks down there to see a badge. Get the chance to express their shock that a 'thing like this' could happen on Shippan Point. Which is probably smart. Because the mood is really hyper down there. The guns are on the nighttables. We'll be lucky to get through this without somebody shooting their dog or their husband who's raiding the fridge."

Stephanie gave a mordant chuckle and opened her eyes wide at Megan. Megan was supposed to comment, or at least to smile, but the corners of her mouth felt frozen. She had come prepared to be questioned across a table with microphones, not to chat. She almost hoped that the investigator would get here quickly.

Stephanie Feltch glanced at her watch, and then got up to look out into the corridor. Returning to her desk, she picked up a pack of cigarettes, but put it down again without taking one. "Well," she said, "did you have a good Thanksgiving?"

Megan's hands clenched in her lap. The question was casual, meaningless, but it was still the state attorney who was asking. "Uh . . . nothing much. I had to work today, so I couldn't go away or anything."

Stephanie Feltch nodded sympathetically. "Same here. I wanted to go up to my parents' but I was on call. See, in Connecticut the rule is that you've got to have an ASA on the scene if it's a felony investigation, so somebody always has to be on call." She shrugged and went on. She seemed to possess in full measure the lawyer's fondness for talking. "Well, obviously, I did get called. There was nothing much to do, but the cops wouldn't let me leave. They kept saying, We'll be bringing the perp in any time. A unit has observed the perp and is in pursuit. That's the way cops talk to you if you're a lawyer, like they're on the stand. So I hung around, trying to avoid going up to the scene. See, I've never been on a homicide before. But when the ME arrived, I figured I better go up with him. You know the worst part? Not the wounds, or the face. I knew enough not to look. It was her hands. They put baggies over her hands. To preserve the scrapings."

Stephanie Feltch was holding up her own hands. Megan tried to keep from staring at them, tried to keep thoughts out of her mind. She concentrated on her own face, on the surface of her skin. But it was impossible to hold in what she was feeling, it was like cupping water in her hands. Something seeped through. She saw the other woman's expression change in response.

"I'm sorry," she said. "You get a little callous in this job. I didn't mean to upset you."

Megan cast about desperately for something to say. "I . . . uh . . . it's just that nothing like this has ever happened to anybody I knew before."

"Sure. It's a terrible shock. Of course, if it had to happen to anybody, you'd just as soon it was Mrs. Elkin, right?"

Megan flinched as if she had been struck. "I don't know what that's supposed to mean."

Stephanie Feltch glanced down at a yellow pad on her desk. It was covered with writing—the notes from her talk with Paul. She read them over, taking her time about it. "Wasn't it because of Mrs. Elkin that you lost your job?"

"I've put all that behind me. I had nothing against Mrs. Elkin."

"Mm. It's probably lawyers that you're fed up with, right? Like you're pretty ticked off at me right now." Again she made that slight movement of her head, to bring her eyes to bear on Megan's. Megan held the look and said nothing. She was angry at Stephanie Feltch; it was the anger that was holding her together.

"The thing I can't figure out is, how could you stand to go back to work for lawyers again?"

"I didn't. I'm a clerk-typist."

"But I thought you were putting together a work sample. To go looking for another para job."

"Oh. Yes. It pays better than what I do now." Megan tried to anticipate the next question: Why did you go into the firm so early? What did you take?

But the assistant state attorney veered unexpectedly. "That company you work for, what do they make?"

"Mailboxes for apartment buildings, mostly."

"You must have a lot of truckers in and out."

"I guess. I don't see them. I'm just in an office."

"Well, when you get out, where do you go? Where do you have lunch? Get a drink after work?"

Now Megan understood, and she was careful to keep the smile off her face, the relief out of her voice. The assistant state's attorney was probing for some connection between her and a thief—probing blindly, because there was no way for her to find it. She said, "I bring lunch. I don't go to bars or anything."

Stephanie Feltch nodded. "Been to New York City lately, Megan?"

Fearful possibilities crowded into Megan's mind—they knew something about the Raymond Gallery, or they had found someone who had seen her on the train, or in the city—and there was no time to think them out. She had to answer. There was no time.

"No. Not for several months."

Stephanie Feltch nodded and glanced at her watch again. "Excuse me for a minute," she said, and got up.

When she was alone, Megan was able to work it out: it was the van Steve had stolen, and abandoned on the scene. It would have had a New York City registration. That was all.

The assistant state's attorney was still probing blindly. She didn't know anything. Megan took a deep breath, uncramped her shoulders.

When Stephanie Feltch returned, she did not sit down. "Look, I'm sorry. I think we're going to have to give up on my investigator. I'll have to ask you to come back next week. I am sorry. I hope you didn't miss your lunch."

She was smiling again; she was back to that flustered cordiality as if nothing had happened between them. She saw Megan out to the waiting room, and shook hands with her. Megan nodded and turned away. She got as far as the staircase before the reaction hit her. Her knees buckled underneath her and she had to grasp the banister and fight for breath. A suspicion lay cold and heavy upon her heart, that Stephanie Feltch had been as false as she. They had not been waiting for the investigator. She had been called in because Stephanie Feltch wanted to get a look at her, to try her out for the part of murderer.

4

She thought, as she returned to the accounting section, that she would have to explain to Pat why she was late. But looking at the clock she saw that she was not late at all. Her lunch hour had a couple of minutes to run. So she had been in Stephanie Feltch's office for only a quarter of an hour. It had seemed so much longer; it was a time that became even more harrowing in her memory. She put it out of her mind. An interval of safety lay before her. Nothing loomed between now and the time of her meeting with Paul.

Going to her desk, she set to work. Megan had never worked so quickly or with such concentration as she did that afternoon. She rapped out the forms, tore out the carbons, filed them away. It gave her satisfaction to slip them into the folders tagged with dates in December and January. The office routine, the laws of this small, sealed-up world, assumed that she would be here to retrieve them, and she felt as if each one was a stitch that bound her to a future. At quitting time, she joined the other women at the coat rack, and joined in the chorus of "See you Monday." Her mind was nestled so comfortably in routine that she started to walk home along her usual route, and had to be called back by the other women, and reminded amid laughs and exclamations that she had brought her car today.

She stepped into her apartment, shut and locked the door behind her. Then she had to brace herself before putting on the light, illuminating the scene of last night: the rope of twisted blanket on the floor, the cup of cold tea, the slate trivet on the end table into which Steve had ground his cigarette butts during their long wait. She had to get rid of all this before Paul got here.

She took the towel Steve had used from the bathroom, and without looking at the stains on it she wrapped it around the whiskey bottle and threw it away. She mopped the kitchen floor and the bathroom, dusted and vacuumed in the living room. She threw away the book she had been reading and the cup she had drunk from. Oddly, it was only when she was finished that she thought of the possibility of the police searching her apartment. Then she put on her coat and went out, taking the trashbag and the vacuum cleaner bag to dispose of them in the dumpster of a big apartment building on the corner.

By the time she got back, she thought that it had to be nearly six. She did not look at the time, though. If it was after six she did not want to know, did not want to wonder why Paul was late, and where he could be. She thought of occupying herself by fixing something to eat, but knew that nothing would go down her throat. She switched off the light and went to the window.

It was the hour of homecoming. The street was busy. Time and again her hopes rose as headlights swept the pavement below, then fell as the car came into view, and was not Paul's. Yet she could not tear herself away from the window. She leaned over until her forehead touched the cold pane of glass, and peered down to the end of the street to catch the first glimpse of him as he turned the corner.

And there he was. She recognized the Saab at once, from the odd shape of its headlights. It moved toward her very slowly, as Paul looked for a parking space along the crowded curbs. She had a moment of frustration so exquisite it almost made her laugh, as if there were no difficulty or danger in the world but for this moment's delay. She couldn't bear it any longer. She went out the door and ran down the stairs, throwing on her coat.

He was just getting out of the car, and as he straightened up she ran to him and embraced him. They hugged each other tightly, closing their arms until they could feel one another's bodies through the thickness of their coats. It was too short a time before Paul said, "We'd better go in."

Holding on to his gloved hand she led him up the stairs. When she let him go to close the door, he wandered away from her into the room. In the light she could see that his face was drawn. Then, for the first time, she thought of what the day had been like for him. He would have had to perform all the executor's duties—make the calls, send out the letters, file the documents—just as if this had been an ordinary decease. And all the time he had been carrying with him his unutterable knowledge of what had really happened. Somehow, knowing what he did, he would have had to talk to the family.

"You don't have to stay, Paul," she said, wretchedly. "I know you shouldn't be here. I just had to see you for a minute. I'll be all right now."

He seemed not to have heard. He paced the room slowly, his hands deep in his overcoat pockets and his face averted. "Meg," he said, "you told me that the—the thief made you drive him back to the city this morning."

"Yes, he did. I don't understand, Paul. Why—"

"Where did you take him?"

"Nowhere. He just told me to drop him off on a streetcorner."

Paul's shoulders sagged as he let out a long breath. "Yeah. I figured it would be something like that."

"Why did you ask?"

"It doesn't matter."

"Why did you ask me that?"

He raised his head and looked at her. Now Megan understood. She said, "Something's happened."

Paul nodded. "I've just come from the state attorney's office. There were some papers Stephanie wanted—"

"She suspects me," Megan interrupted. "I already know that. I could see it this afternoon."

"No, it's nothing like that. It's got nothing to do with you."

"How can it be nothing to do with me?"

"It's the thief. The cops got a break. They got a lead to him." Paul's face twisted up with bitterness. "I walked into this big celebration. Stephanie was passing out beers from the fridge. She couldn't wait to tell me all about it. She said the cops were checking out that van—the one the thief abandoned at the scene—"

"It won't do them any good. It's not his. He told me that. He stole it, and he had gloves on the whole time he was in it."

"Under the seat they found a road map of Stamford. Since the owner of the van lives in Queens, they figure it must have been the thief's."

"Maybe. So what?"

"Stephanie said to me, 'Have you ever tried to unfold a road map with gloves on?' "

Megan sat down on the couch, so that her back was to him. She said nothing.

"The cops got really lucky, according to Stephanie. Paper doesn't take fingerprints very well. But this was one of those Hagstrom maps, with a cover that had some kind of slick coating. They were able to lift a full set of clear prints."

When she remained silent, he came around and sat on the couch beside her. He leaned forward, studying her face, but Megan could not look at him. She said, "They're going to get him."

"They're a long way from that, Meg. They haven't even identified him yet. There's a computer in Washington that searches arrest records and matches prints, but you have to wait a long time to get to use it."

"But they're not going to wait. Are they?"

"No. They're trying something else.

"What?"

"It won't necessarily work."

"What are they trying to do?"

"They've sent some detectives down to New York. Apparently the precincts there keep what they call known burglar files. The detectives are going through those files, trying to match the prints. But he may not even be in any of the files."

"I know he's been in jail. He told me that. So there's a record of him someplace."

"They may not find the record. Even if they can identify him, they've still got to catch him."

"Catch him? But he's not running. He's not hiding. He thinks there's nothing for him to worry about." Her voice broke, as she remembered Steve telling her how he had made no mistakes. "If they do get him, what then?"

"Stephanie didn't tell me anything about that." Paul sighed heavily. "But I know how prosecutors operate. They'll offer him a deal—a lighter sentence if he'll testify against his accomplice. I suppose there's no reason to think that he wouldn't name you."

"No. If they get him, they'll get me."

"Meg, none of this is certain." He reached out to embrace her and draw her to him, but she pushed his arms away and stood up.

"You asked me where I took him this morning. Why?"

"That was nothing. That was just a crazy idea."

"You thought if I knew where he lived that I could get a warning to him." She still had her coat on, and she patted her pockets to make sure her keys were there. "I've got to try," she said. "I've got to go now."

Paul rose too. "Do you know some way of getting in touch—?"

"I know his first name. I can find the corner where I let him off." Paul was staring at her, shaking his head. But Megan was thinking of the way Steve had said, "This is close enough." Close enough to what? She took her shoulder bag from the chair and turned to the door.

Paul said, "Meg, wait. This just isn't possible."

"I've got to try."

"All right. I'm coming with you."

"No. If I find him, there can't be anyone with me."

"At least let me drive you—"

"No. You can't be with me. You can't take the risk." She swung around to face him. "What you've done already, telling me all this—it's worse than holding back information. It's made you an accomplice, hasn't it?"

He did not seem to hear her. "When you get back, come straight to my place. Whatever happens, come to me." He held her face in both his hands, and kissed her mouth. Then he let her go.

5

The drive seemed to take much longer than it had in the morning, and there was a mile-long crawl to the bridge tolls. At last she got through and accelerated. She looked out the side window and saw far off to the west the cluster of glittering spikes that was midtown Manhattan. Ahead of her, as she crested the long sloping arch of the bridge, there was only a vast maze made up of points of light—yellow, white, green, red. She could not recognize any pattern of streets, could not descry any buildings. Would she even remember the exit Steve had told her to take? The street sign had been covered with graffiti, obliterating the name.

But only a few miles from the bridge the highway bore left in a sweeping curve, and there was an exit ramp leading down to the right. The configuration jogged something in her memory. This was it.

At the bottom she knew to turn left. It was a broad, dark, featureless street which had not registered on her mind at all. She drove along slowly, peering out, as cars honked and swept past her. Ahead there was a stoplight, and, crossing over the intersection, the girders of an elevated subway. This was where Steve had gotten out of the car.

She pulled over and parked, then walked to the corner around which he had disappeared, and looked down the street. There was nothing to give her hope: only the gargantuan rib-cage of steel uprights, and the black, hulking walls of factories and warehouses. She started walking. A cold, gusting wind blew grit in her face, sent newspaper pages sailing, stirred the eddies of litter in the angles of the building. People coming toward her had their shoulders hunched, their heads bent. They looked wretched, furtive; if she approached them they would snap at her, like stray dogs. She was going to have to talk to a lot of people tonight. If she could find anyone to ask.

There was a thundering overhead. A train went clanking and pounding by. Its wheels screeched as it went into a turn, and she watched as the line of lights curved with the tracks, then were swallowed up by the darkness. Steve could have gotten on the subway. He could be anywhere in the city by now.

No, she thought. If she knew nothing else about him, not his last name or his address, she knew a little of his moods. If he'd wanted to get away from her he would have had her drop him far to the north, at the first subway in the Bronx. But he had been ebullient and careless, and in a hurry. It was only at the last moment that he'd decided not to have her take him right to his destination. "This is close enough."

She came to an intersection. Looking to the left she saw lighted windows and neon signs, a line of cars waiting at the signal, people on the sidewalks. The other way, there was only the gray sheen of streetlamps on empty pavement, and rows of squat, dark apartment houses. They would confront her with locked lobby doors and a row of last names on mailboxes. She turned away and headed for the lights.

On the corner was the narrow, gaudy frontage of a newsstand. It had a big sign advertising a brand of cigarettes. She remembered something: Steve, in the car this morning, wadding up his empty pack of cigarettes and throwing it out the window. He was a chain smoker. He wouldn't have gone far without cigarettes. As long a shot as it was, it gave her a surge of hope, and she went in.

The place was no more than a narrow aisle between racks of magazines. At the end, beneath a hanging fringe of girlie magazines, a jowly, bespectacled man sat at a cash register. There were no other customers, but he did not look at Megan as she entered. She went up to him and said good evening. He glanced at her hands, empty of purchases, and then, suspiciously, at her face.

"I wonder if you can help me. I'm trying to find a guy named Steve. He may have been in here this morning. A young guy, stocky, with blond hair."

The man ducked his head and peered at her, but said nothing.

"I . . . uh, I gave him a ride this morning. Picked him up hitchhiking. I dropped him off at the corner here. Then I realized he'd left something in the car. Now I'm trying to find him."

"So how come you think he came in here?" he demanded.

"I don't know if he did or not. But he may have come in to buy cigarettes."

The man frowned. He shifted his bulk on the high stool, and shook his head so vigorously that the points of light danced on his glasses. "So what if he did, I'm supposed to remember every guy who comes in here to buy cigarettes all day? What time was this?"

"It would have been a little after seven this morning."

"Seven in the morning I'm not even open. Seven in the morning, morning after Thanksgiving, practically nobody around here's open. What d'you expect?" He heaved himself off the stool, turned away, and began noisily throwing magazines around.

Megan sighed and headed for the door. This first attempt had been even worse than she'd expected; she should have known. The more desperate you were, the more harshly New York would deal with you. People here were insulted by a request for help. They had to crush you for asking. She could only go on to the next place, hope for better there. But even as her hand closed on the door handle, she could feel the man's words working on her: practically nobody around here's open. It would be hard to go on. It would be so much easier to give up, once she walked out of here. She turned and went back to the man.

"Excuse me."

He kept his back to her. "Lady, unless you want to buy something—"

"All right. I do." She dug in her purse and slapped a five-dollar bill down on the counter. She kept her hand on it. "Who is open at that time of the day?"

He had turned to face her, hands in his pockets, head thrown back. Now he started to turn away.

"I'm buying an answer. Just tell me one thing and I'll give you five bucks and leave, all right? If a guy wanted to get a pack of cigarettes at seven in the morning around here, where would he go? Who's open before you are?"

He made a chopping motion of his arm. She thought at first he was waving her away, but then he said, "Up the next corner there's a place. Guy who owns it is a raghead, and he's open all the fucking time." His jowls rippled; Megan realized it wasn't the money that made him talk, it was the chance to vent a grudge. "He's got his whole family working for him. He's open, even if he's got to send in his little kid or his grandmother."

Megan turned and left the shop. The direction the man had indicated was back the way she had come. She recrossed the street and passed along the row of apartment buildings. On the corner was the small shopfront, and as she drew nearer she could read the hand-lettered sign in the window: *Alterations! Copying! Do you need cigarettes? Or candy? Welcome in!*

The place was a warren of racks lined with miscellaneous merchandise, and as Megan went through her questions and explanations to the man at the counter, members of the family kept appearing to stand before her. The eyes in the dark faces looked wide and apprehensive, and no one said anything. Megan wondered if they did not know English well enough to understand her, or if the questions frightened them.

When she finished there were sidelong glances, then the little knot of people parted and a slender youth was moved to the fore. He was grave and handsome, with the thin, glossy black mustache of a thirties movie star.

"You were on this morning?" Megan guessed.

He nodded. "Yes, from six to ten only I was here."

"Do you remember a man coming in to buy cigarettes around seven? A young man, stocky, with blue eyes and blond hair?"

He gave a delicate shudder of his shoulders. "There are so many faces—"

"Yes, I understand." Megan shut her eyes and reached back in her memory. If only she could recall what brand Steve smoked. Only a few hours ago she had been gathering up the butts he'd left in her apartment, and she had not noticed. But there was one thing she did remember about them. She raised her eyes to her patient audience. "He smokes the kind with no filters. Lucky Strike, or Camel, or—"

"Chesterfield, no filter." The man was nodding vigorously. "Yes, yes. It took some minutes to find them. I remember that man." He gave a few more nods in silence, then added, "I thought he must be going somewhere nearby."

"You saw which way he went?" Megan was almost dizzy with her good fortune.

"No, I'm sorry, but it must be somewhere nearby. He had no coat. In his shirtsleeves only. And it's bloody cold, you know."

There was no doubt it was Steve, with his jacket bundled under his arm. "Where could he have gone? What's around here?"

Another slight, regretful shrug. "Apartment houses."

Megan tried to ignore the possibility that Steve had vanished into that forbidding row behind her. "What's in the other direction? Are there shops or cafeterias, anything that would have been open?"

He thought a moment. "There is the gas station. And the

laundromat." He looked from side to side, and received only nods; he must have covered all the possibilities.

Megan was filled with hope. "Thank you," she said. "Thank you. You've been a great help." No one answered; no one moved as she turned away, and she heard no sound behind her. She had the feeling still that she had given them some sort of scare. She did not know if, once the door had shut behind her, they would begin talking, speculating, or if they would go about their business as if nothing had happened.

A gas station or a laundromat. The former seemed a better possibility. She knew at least that Steve had a car. She walked on until she came to it. There was no one at the pumps so she went into the office. A couple of teenage boys lounged in the doorway to the garage, drinking Cokes; another boy in a base-ball cap sat at the desk reading a magazine.

"Excuse me."

The bill of the cap tipped up and the boy glanced at her, then out the door. He was looking for her car.

"I'm looking for a guy named Steve."

"Steve," he echoed. The boys at the door had stopped talking and were looking at her.

Megan pressed on. "Young guy, blond hair. He drives an old yellow car—a two-seater. Maybe a Fiat, or an MG . . ."

The boy's eyes were narrowed and his mouth hung open.

There was a ringing laugh from the back of the room, and one of the boys in the doorway swaggered toward her, open-ing his arms. "Hey, my name's Steve."

"Don't listen to him," said the other, grinning. "His name's Tony."

"Nah, I'm Steve. I'm the man you're looking for."

"His name's fuckface," the other cried out, and they both laughed.

Megan looked down at the boy at the desk. "Please," she said.

But with his friends laughing behind him, he decided he had better laugh at her too. Megan turned away and went out.

"Hey, don't go," a voice called out. "You can call me Steve if that's what turns you on."

"She don't want you, fuckface, she wants Steve." Megan looked over her shoulder. They were all spilling out the door.

She swung round to face them, but they did not approach. One threw back his head and called out, "Steve! Where are ya?"

Megan turned and hurried away, as the ragged, derisive chorus of voices bellowed "Steve!" behind her. She ran across the street and down a line of darkened buildings, until she was out of earshot. Then she stopped, gasping, and leaned against the wall.

Fatigue and hopelessness came up at her in a black wave. This was stupid. Futile. She was never going to find him. He had bought his pack of cigarettes and turned an undiscoverable corner and gone an unknowable distance to one of those long bulwarks of apartment houses. He could be found only by ringing countless doorbells, asking endless questions. That was something the police could do, but she could not. Perhaps they had started already. Perhaps, if she went on, she would blunder into their path.

Come to my place, Paul had said. Come straight to me, however it turns out. He had known she could not do this, and he was right. She would return to her car and go to him. He would not abandon her because she'd failed, but comfort her and . . .

Megan put her hands against the rough brick wall and pushed herself away from it. Aloud she said, "He can't help you." She repeated the words. This was something she had to make herself accept. Paul could do nothing more for her. If she did not find Steve the police would, and then they would get her. If she gave up she was finished.

She wiped the weak tears away with her gloved hand and drove herself out into the wind.

The laundromat was just a few doors down. It was a big place, warm and smelling strongly of soap, and there were a lot of people tending the machines or sitting on the plastic chairs along the wall. Methodically, doggedly, Megan began to talk to them. She had no idea what could have brought Steve here; she was past thinking, really, and all she could do was ask. She talked to a pretty, olive-skinned girl who kept smiling and turning away, in embarrassment; to an older woman who was nervous and indignant, as if Megan were begging for money; to a man who was friendly and curious, and put her to the trouble of elaborating on her story of why she was trying to find Steve, before admitting that he couldn't help her at all.

Megan sank down in a chair. There were other customers, further back along the rows of gleaming machines, and she would talk to them too, in a minute. She was very tired, and the warm soapy air and the sound of churning water were soporific. She noticed a row of vending machines on the opposite wall. She got up and dug for change in her pockets.

It was when she was standing in front of the coffee machine that she saw the bulletin board. She moved closer and began to read the little scraps of paper. Things for sale, babysitting and language lessons offered, pleas for the return of lost objects. A vague hope stirred in Megan. She kept on looking, and came upon a few messages that were personal and immediate—reminders or invitations to meet, from one person to another. None of the names was Steve, but he would have taken the message with him, wouldn't he, if this morning he had come in here.

She walked to the back of the laundromat. There was a small office, where a black man with grizzled hair and bright steel spectacles was loudly stacking baskets. He had on a white shirt heavily stained with sweat. Megan stood before him for a while, and when he took no notice of her, she took a ten dollar bill out and put it down on the counter between them. Still without looking at her, the man slapped a roll of quarters down beside the bill.

"It's not for change. I want to—"

"I don't know Steve, and that's free."

"Oh," Megan said. "You noticed."

"Sure did." He had a deep, humorous voice. "Last time I saw something like that, it was on the TV. We get the cops in here, we get them plenty, but you're something else. You some kind of a private eye?"

"No, nothing like that. I just wanted to ask you about your board—"

"Oh, man, I saw you looking at it, and I just knew you'd be over to bug me about it. More trouble than it's worth. It was here when I took over the place. I tried taking it down, but people only pinned things to the walls. Now it's back, but they're not satisfied. They call up. Luther, they say, you don't mind putting a note up on that board of yours, do you? Just write down for Joanne that she better pick up something from the market, 'cause her mom's coming over for dinner." He shrugged and went on with his stacking. "What can I do? This ain't Forest Hills. People round here don't have a answering service or a beeper or stuff like that."

Megan had listened attentively to the man, and she recognized that he was someone like herself—a kindred, put-upon spirit. "You don't know Steve, but you know whoever it is who leaves messages for him, don't you?"

For the first time, he paused in his stacking. Then he went on, shaking his head. "Hey, maybe you are a private eye, huh?"

"You know I'm not. If I were, I'd be better at this. Nobody hired me to do this. I'm not from any agency that will give you trouble. I'm just somebody who's got to find Steve." She tried to meet the man's eye. "The person who leaves messages for him—she'd want me to find him. She or he."

He didn't look at her, but the pace of his stacking slowed with consideration. "All right. I do know her. Or him. Only how do I know that what you're telling me is true?"

"Do you really want me to explain it to you?"

"No." He chuckled richly. "No, that I don't need." He stopped his sorting and laid his hands flat on the counter. He gave her a long look.

"All right," he said at last. "Here's what you do. Go out on this street, walk up a few blocks. There's a McDonald's. Get yourself a coffee or something, have a seat. At the front, near the door."

"Then what?"

"That's up to her. Or him."

It was the best she could expect, and she started to turn away.

"Hey, you forgot this." The man gave her back her ten, and returned to his work before she could thank him.

6

The McDonald's stood at the corner of a wide, busy street. It was a large one, with a playground in front surrounded by a high fence. A line of cars, lights on and engines thrumming, waited at the take-out windows, but the bright interior with its rows of shiny tables was almost empty. Megan got her cup of coffee and walked back to a table near the front door, just as Luther had directed.

For what seemed a long time she sat looking at the traffic that passed beyond her own shadowy reflection in the window. She felt exposed sitting in this bright cube. She was, of course: Luther had sent her here to be seen and evaluated by Steve's girlfriend. That it was the girlfriend was only a guess, but one she felt sure of. It all depended on the girl out in the darkness somewhere.

A police car went slowly past in the street. The New York police cars were smaller than the Stamford ones, and had brighter paintwork. They were almost like toys in comparison. The twinge of fear it gave Megan was like the pains she sometimes felt in a finger she had broken years ago: something familiar and small, something that would always be with her. She wondered if the men in that car had a description or a photo of Steve. If the hunt had begun by now. Then she stopped thinking about it. She was just too tired now. She took another sip of the coffee, but it had grown cold.

A cleaner was slowly making the round of the place. When he got to her Megan lifted her feet for his mop, but did not pay him any attention until he took the still half-full cup off the table and threw it away. She glanced up at him.

"Go 'cross the street. B&R Lounge."

Megan nodded. She went out into the cold again. Directly across the street was a squiggle of neon spelling B&R. She waited for a gap in traffic and crossed.

It was a big, plain building isolated between fenced-in parking lots. As she drew nearer she could hear the rock beat from inside, like a fusillade of blows. Colored lights glowed from the small windows. She was a few steps from the door when a girl's voice called out, "Hey!"

Megan turned and saw an indistinct figure at the edge of the building. She walked over, and when she drew near the girl turned her back and went through a side door. Megan followed.

It was a narrow, empty corridor. The bang and clatter from the kitchen overwhelmed the roar of the music. The girl was small and dark-haired, and wore a waitress's uniform. She hoisted herself up on the counter and sat with her head down, waiting.

"I have to find Steve. It's very important."

"Yeah. Well, he ain't around here."

Megan took a step closer. "You've got to contact him right away. The police are going to be looking for him. If they aren't already."

"So what'm I supposed to do about it?"

"Don't you understand?" Megan asked incredulously. "You've got to warn him right away."

The girl did not reply, but at least she raised her head. Beneath her short, teased hair she had a low forehead, broad cheekbones, and a chin that came to a sharp point. The skin was taut over the bones, the complexion sallow beneath her makeup. It looked honed-down, that face, as if any soft surplus had been worn away. She had on short black pants and a dark-toned top that was as sheer as her tights. You could see her breasts but you also saw her collarbone and the muscles of her shoulders. It would take a very drunk man, Megan thought, in a very dim light, to find that lean torso soft and alluring.

141

"So who are you?" the girl said.

"My name is—"

"Not your name. Just what do you got to do with Steve?"

"I was the one who set up the—the job Steve was on last night. In Connecticut."

"Uh-uh," the girl interrupted. "Steve couldn't've been on no job last night. 'Cause when he's got money he don't sit on it like some guys. After he's done a job we party."

"My God," Megan murmured. "You don't know. He didn't tell you what happened last night."

"Steve don't tell me his business," the girl said. She dropped her head again, but now Megan had the sense that she was waiting, listening.

"There was no money because the job went wrong. The owner of the house was there. She came on Steve by surprise, and he panicked. He killed her."

The girl showed no reaction at all, at first. Then, slowly, she began to shake her head. "No. No, I'm not gonna buy any of this shit. 'Cause, like, I know the only person Steve's got a deal going with is a guy. I seen him. This Soho guy with pink sunglasses. You, I don't know nothing about you."

Megan shut her eyes in frustration. This couldn't happen. She couldn't have come so far only to be thwarted by the girl's obdurate stupidity. "It happened. He's wanted for murder. The police have got his name, or they will soon. Then they'll come looking for him. He's got to get out of town. If you don't warn him they'll get him." The girl just went on shaking her head, like some sort of mechanical doll. "You know where he is, don't you? Take me to him. I'll talk to him myself."

The girl's head came up sharply, as if she had been waiting for this. She slipped down from the counter and grasped both Megan's arms. The movement was not quick, but still it took Megan by surprise, and she did not resist. The girl walked her backward into the corner. Then she reached under her coat and blouse. The small cold hands with their sharp nails moved over her ribcage, the cups of her bra, the waistband of her slacks. All the time, the flat dark eyes stayed fixed on Megan's own.

"I'm not carrying a weapon."

"I'm looking for a wire," the girl said.

142

"I'm not carrying a weapon," Megan repeated, not understanding.

The girl smirked. "A *wire*. A bug. A listening device, understand?"

"No. Why would I have—"

"There a bunch of cops outside? Waiting while you talk me into taking you to Steve? Waiting to follow us?"

"Good God—don't you understand? I'm trying to warn him, trying to keep us both out of jail."

The girl withdrew her hands from Megan's body and straightened up. "That's good. You want to stay out of jail, lady. You didn't like me touching you, did you? Well, that's nothing to what they do to you in jail. In jail they make you strip and you take your showers in a big room with a bunch of guards watching. Then you line up naked with your arms up in the air, and you all file past this guard who sprays you with deodorant. See, they won't let you have deodorant yourself. And that's only the beginning. That's before they lock you up in the cell and walk away. Leave you with whatever's in there."

The girl's voice and face had changed as she spoke; softened. Trying to frighten Megan, she had frightened herself. Megan repeated, "I'm trying to keep us both out of jail."

The girl's eyes were still fixed on hers. "All that stuff you been telling me—the job and the killing and all—that's true?"

"Yes."

Abruptly the girl turned away. She was back in a moment, pulling on a jacket. "Come on."

They went out to the parking lot. The girl bent to unlock a car door. It was the yellow two-seater. Megan looked at it warily. "Is this registered to Steve? The police may—"

"No. It's mine," the girl said, as if Megan had threatened to take it away from her.

They got into the car. Megan asked, "Where is Steve?"

"My place. Near that laundromat. Not far." Slipping off her high heels, she started the car and drove out into the street.

"Would the police know to come looking for him there?"

"Uh-uh. No way." The girl kept a troubled silence for a moment. Then she said, "Larry, this jerk that's my probation officer, he knows. My mom told him or something. He comes down on me real hard for seeing Steve. He gets me in there and, like, reads Steve's yellow sheet to me. Like I'm not supposed to know he's been in the joint. Like that's supposed to scare me off."

"Would he tell the police about you and Steve?"

"I don't know." A moment later she said, "Yeah. He'd tell 'em."

They were both silent after that. The girl was a poor driver; the car kept weaving slightly, its speed dropping off and picking up. She drove like a sixteen-year-old on a learner's permit, and Megan wondered how old she was.

They turned into a narrow, rutted alley, and parked behind a row of looming apartment buildings. The girl led the way up a long zigzag of fire-escape steps. At the top she unlocked a door. Rock music poured out as she opened it.

"Steve?"

"Yeah?" he yelled from another room. "You back already, Marla?"

The girl glanced at Megan and then crossed the room to go through a doorway with a beaded curtain. Megan stayed where she was, for she had understood the glance: I need a minute to work this out with *him*. It was a message that one woman always understood from another, even two women who had as little in common as she and Marla.

From where she stood she could see all of the cramped room. A paper shade over the light fixture cast a pink glow over the cracked plaster and mottled carpeting. The kitchen appliances were lined up on the wall to her right. There was also the stereo with its tall speakers, a big television set, and other electronics that she supposed Marla owed to Steve's talents. The furniture, though, was scanty and cheap.

Steve burst through the beaded curtains and stood glaring across the room at her. His T-shirted chest swelled with slow, angry breathing. Marla came back and turned the record player off. "She says—"

"That's about the dumbest thing you coulda done, bringing her here."

Marla flinched and looked down. She said in a small hard voice, "You didn't tell me it was a killing this time."

Steve's face went white and he flung out an arm rigidly,

to point at Megan. "That's her goddam fault. She guaranteed me the place would be empty, so I wasn't expecting nothing."

Megan could not bear to hear that again. She said, "There isn't much time. They're going to find out your name, if they haven't got it already. They're going to come looking for you."

"No way they've got anything on me. I didn't make no mistakes. I didn't fuck up. The only fuck-up on this job was you."

"You had a map. You left it behind under the seat." There was a momentary flicker in his eyes as he remembered. "It had your fingerprints on it. They're going around the precincts now trying to match those prints. If they haven't identified you already."

"So they're going around every precinct house in the whole city—that what you come to tell me? So around Christmastime I'll start to worry."

"They'll probably start with the precinct where the van was reported stolen," Marla said. "Work out from there. That would make sense."

Megan looked at her in surprise: it did make sense. But she seemed afraid to ask the next question. Megan said: "Where did you get the van?"

Steve dropped his head and hooked his thumbs in his belt loops. "I went and got the van on fucking Staten Island, what do you think?" His lips worked for a minute, then he said, "I picked it up over on Twenty-ninth."

"But that's only a coupla—" Steve turned his back on Marla, so she spoke to Megan. "The cops around here, they been trying to pin some stuff on Steve. Had him in for a standup just last week."

Steve rounded on her. "Shut up! Just shut up! I never should've told you about that."

In the same small, steady voice, Marla said, "You got to run, Steve."

"All right. All right. I'll go down to that place of Frank's, down—" He hesitated, remembering Megan. "That place we went last summer. For a while. Nobody'll think of looking for me there. It worked last time."

"Last time you just missed a court appearance on a possession-of-burglar's-tools rap. It was just a sheriff coming around.

This time they're not going to give up. They're going to lean on everybody who knows you. You can't go to that place Frank has. You got to get out of the city. You killed somebody, Steve."

She had gotten through to him at last. His lips were clenched and his head made small, jerky movements. His eyes came to bear upon Megan.

"Marla, step out for a minute," he said. The girl rose and slipped through the curtains carefully, so that the beads hardly swayed behind her. It was her meekness that made the fear stir in Megan.

Steve began to walk toward her, speaking softly.

"You think I'm going to run, just 'cause you say so? I don't buy any of this. What really happened is the cops pulled you in. Told you they almost had me, threw a scare into you. And you got so scared you came running down here. Right?"

"You know it's true about the map. You remember that."

"If this was true there's no fucking way the cops would tell you about it. They'd tell you only if they was making it up."

"It's true. I didn't get it from the—" Steve's hand came up at her. She ducked her head to avoid a blow, but there was no blow. Instead he dug his fingers into her hair and clenched them.

He twisted and pulled forward and down, very slowly. She had to bend over, then had to drop to her knees. He kept on twisting, turning her head. She could see him. He was gazing at her as if her face, in a rictus of pain, were an object of rare beauty. He wasn't going to stop. The realization filled her with a horror that made the pain as nothing, and with a sudden, tearing jerk, she pulled free. Got to her feet, got her back against the wall.

He took a step toward her.

"Don't come near me."

A moment, and then Steve backed away, spreading his arms, opening his hands. A few strands of her hair drifted to the carpet. "Okay," he said. "Just tell me where you got your information, okay?"

Megan did not answer. She was breathing hard and her heart was pounding. Her whole frame was shaking—not trembling, but vibrating with leashed-in energy. Her fingers had curled into claws. She knew that if Steve had come a step nearer she would have leapt at him and dug for his eyes. She had not decided it; no thought had been involved. But she knew what she would have done. Now, deliberately, she made her fingers relax.

"Hey, I'm not going to get near you. Okay?" The hushed tension was gone from Steve's voice. He was grinning. Having hurt her, he didn't feel so scared anymore. "Just tell me. Where'd you get this story?"

She longed to get out of this place, to turn and walk away. She could hardly bear to look at him. But it had to be done. He had to be convinced.

"It's true. It's from the state attorney's office. It was told to someone I know, someone I can trust. And he passed it on to me."

Steve was baffled for a moment, then, slowly, he began to nod. "It's that lawyer guy, right? Got to be. The old lady's lawyer. The one you were so sure was gonna figure out what you did and run to the cops. Only he didn't. Just like I said. He kept his mouth shut. And now he's helping you out, right?"

It filled Megan with disgust that he should have guessed this. "I've got nothing else to say to you. If you don't believe me you can go to hell."

"Oh, lady, I believe you. I'm just not used to people taking so much trouble over me. I'm not used to being so important." He grinned and turned away. "Hey, Marla!"

She came back through the doorway so quickly that she must have been waiting just out of sight. She looked not at Steve but at Megan, with an expression that was unreadable.

"Need some money," Steve said. "I'm going out of town for a while."

The girl went to the refrigerator, knelt to rummage among the vegetables, and came up with a fold of bills. Steve took them and riffled through them. "That all?"

Marla nodded.

He turned to Megan. "How 'bout you? What you got?"

She made no reply.

"Hey. You want me out of town, right? You want me to go real far, real fast. Right? So it's going to cost you."

She hesitated. But then she reached into her purse for her

147

wallet. Steve took it from her, pulled out all the bills and emptied the change into his hand. He dropped the wallet onto the floor.

"Wait a minute. Leave me some change, I've got to get over the bridge . . ."

Steve might not have heard her. He was pulling on his jacket, checking his pockets. "Need a ride to the bus station," he said to Marla, and walked out the door.

Megan bent to pick up her wallet. She was on the fire escape when Marla caught up with her. The girl slipped something into her hand and went on by. Megan stopped and looked: there were four dollar bills, all crumpled up like the money a child hoards away.

7

The door opened as she came up to it. Paul had been watching for her. He held out his arms and she stepped into them. Neither one spoke. She gripped him tightly as he drew her into his house.

She struggled out of her coat and let it fall, and sank down into the nearest chair. She was exhausted. The drive back, with the streetlamps unfurling endlessly ahead of her, and the big trucks rushing past, had used up the last of her strength. Only the bite of that cup of coffee she'd drunk in the McDonald's had kept her awake. Paul came to kneel on the floor in front of her. He took off her shoes and socks, and began to rub her feet. He still had said nothing to her, had asked no questions, and she realized that he was assuming that she had failed.

She said, "I found him. I talked him into leaving. He's long gone by now, I suppose."

Paul's face came up. "You *found* him?"

She nodded.

Paul rocked back on his haunches, clapped his hands together, and gave a shout of fierce exultation. It was the sort of thing he used to do when his old college team scored a goal in hockey, and she looked at him in bewilderment.

"Meg—my God—you did it. You're safe now."

"Safe," Megan echoed. She supposed that it was true, and if she said the word perhaps it would mean something to her. "Safe."

Paul was still grinning and shaking his head. His face was flushed with his happiness and relief. "How on earth—I mean, you started on a streetcorner in Queens, knowing nothing about the guy but his first name, and you *found* him? I never thought you could do it. I couldn't've done it in a million years."

Megan thought that this was true. Paul was not shy, but he had no skill for talking to strangers. He couldn't have done it. Throughout their lives together, she had either followed in his footsteps or gotten in his way, at the office, on the boat, on the trail. Now she had done something he couldn't.

"How?" he asked. "How did you do it?"

Megan tried to gather her thoughts to make some sort of answer. But it was a jumble—the cold gritty wind, the glare and blackness of the streets, all those strangers' faces. Steve's face, above her, gazing rapt upon her pain. When she had gotten back to the car the first thing she had done was to look in the driving mirror. She had expected to see blood and a patch of bare scalp. But to her relief there had been no sign. She wasn't going to tell Paul about that. She didn't want to tell him anything. She said, "I was scared. That's how I could do it."

Paul was grave now. He stood and covered both her hands with his own. "There's nothing to be scared of now. Without the thief, they'll never be able to put together a case against you."

149

"It was a bad thing to do," Megan said.

"Sure. You've had an awful night. You don't have to tell me. Try to forget about it."

"I don't mean that. I mean that it was—it was *vile*, having to help that man get away so he wouldn't get the chance to betray me."

"It wasn't any of your doing, Meg. The law ties you to him." He bent close to her, his eyes searching her face. "All that matters is you're in the clear now. You did it. Please, Meg, be happy." He stood, abruptly. "You're tired. You're hungry. Have you had anything at all to eat today?"

She shook her head. Paul turned purposefully to the kitchen. She tried to call him back, saying that she didn't think she could eat anything. But he paid no attention. And it was oddly soothing to hear him rummaging around in there.

She sat upright. There was no reason to sit huddled in the chair; it was as warm here as a summer's day with all the windows open. Even her bare feet weren't chilly. She curled her toes in the dense pile of the carpet. The cushions were firm and plump beneath her. Now she began to look about this familiar apartment, which she had not seen in so long. Her eye took in the shine of polished wood, and the deeper luster of leather, and the vibrant hues of the Persian rug. There were net curtains drawn over the big windows at the end of the room. Beyond lay the darkness of the harbor and the sea. The lights in the houses on the opposite shore were as remote as stars. It was so quiet here. She might have been all alone in the world with Paul.

I'm back. I'm safe, she thought, trying it out.

When he returned carrying a big tray cocooned in foil, she knew what to expect. Paul was always going to parties where the hosts were solicitous of a bachelor, and his refrigerator held caterer's leftovers even if it held nothing else. He put the tray down, and stood back with his hands in his front pockets, beaming uncertainly down at her. So there was nothing for her to do but try to eat.

The crust was so dry that she could hardly swallow her first bite of *pâté en croûte*, but at the second bite the rich taste of the meat roused her appetite. She began to eat ravenously, of limp asparagus wrapped in desiccated prosciutto, of rubbery deviled eggs filled with caviar, of flaking cheddar and gooey Brie on hard bread. Leaving the tray bare, she leaned back. She was going to get a bad case of indigestion for this. It amused her that she should be worried about such a thing. Seeing her smile, Paul smiled back.

"You look like you're about to drop off."

"If only I didn't have to wake up and drive."

"Don't. Stay here."

Megan sat upright. What had she meant by that remark—had she meant to draw such an invitation from him? No, it wasn't that. She had fallen into her old habit with Paul, of speaking whatever was in her mind. She had spoken without thinking. That was a luxury she could not afford. She bent over and began to put on her socks and shoes.

"No. I'd better get home."

"Are you sure?"

"I shouldn't stay here too long."

"No," he said, "I suppose not."

But when she got up he rose with her and took her in his arms. It was swift, instinctive, as if a fragile object were falling to the floor and he moved to catch it. She thought it could not hurt to hold him for a moment before she left. She wrapped her arms around his back, and laid her head against his chest. There was a nook, where the broad ledge of his collarbone met the smooth, rounded muscle of his shoulder, that fit her forehead perfectly. The beat of his heart filled her ear. Her head moved slightly with his breathing. Deep within her Megan felt a small, hot stitch of wanting.

Paul said, "Please don't go."

Without breaking the embrace, she straightened up so that she could meet his eyes. She saw in them what she felt. She took his hands and laid them upon her breasts, then knit her fingers together behind his neck and brought his mouth down to hers.

After a time they broke away so that they could undress. She bent to untie the shoes she had just tied. She remembered how they used to laugh at moments like this. The memory pleased her, but she did not laugh now. Her clothes seemed heavy and clinging, her fingers clumsy. It was like stripping after being drenched in a rainstorm. She shed each garment with relief.

At last they sank to the carpet naked, and she opened her body under his. She was so pliant she could not feel him enter her as she wanted to. She put her hands on his buttocks and pressed, crooked her legs over his knees. She held him still inside her for a long moment. Then she set him free. Their bodies moved together, and Megan drifted away where her thoughts could not reach her any more, where nothing could reach her but wave upon wave of pleasure.

She came back to herself slowly. Paul was saying they should go to bed. They left their clothes behind and went up the stairs with their arms around one another. That too was something they had done before. Even as she slipped into the big bed Megan was falling asleep, her first real sleep in many nights.

PART IV

1

She came back into the room and stood at the foot of the bed. Paul was breathing deeply and evenly: he was still asleep. Her eyes grew accustomed to the darkness and she could see him. His arms were outflung as if he were still holding her. She had been careful not to wake him when she had gotten out of bed a few minutes ago. In the past, they used to move apart after making love, turn their backs to one another. It was more comfortable not to have the other's limbs weighing upon one, the other's hair in one's face. But that was in the days when they had taken things for granted. Last night she had slept in his arms.

She said his name, and he stirred, then sat upright. He

peered at her, seeing that she was fully dressed. "Oh no," he said. "Couldn't you sleep?"

"I slept wonderfully. Thank you. But I have to go now."

"Not yet."

"Yes. It's later than it seems. The day's just dark." She found that she was gripping the bedstead tightly. She let go. "Your phone's been ringing."

"The machine takes care of it."

"People are expecting you places. You have things to do."

"It doesn't matter."

"Paul, it does."

"All right. I'll call you later on, when—"

She interrupted. "What do you think is going to happen today?"

"Probably nothing. It's Saturday."

"You think they won't have me in for questioning until next week?"

He rubbed his face with both hands and cleared his throat. He did not want to answer.

"They haven't even begun to question me yet, not really. Yesterday that woman—Stephanie Feltch—she was just toying with me. She things I'm guilty. She wants to get me."

"Meg, don't make it personal. It's not. Stephanie is not a bad person. She just wants to do her job well. They don't get many murders in Stamford and she wants to make the most of this one."

"When she was questioning me it seemed pretty damn personal."

"When they've got you in there, if things start to get bad, stop answering them." His voice sounded alert and forceful, as his professional self came to the fore. "For some reason it's easier to tell a lie than to keep silent. But keeping silent is what you have to do. If things get bad, Meg, say you want a lawyer before you'll answer any more questions. Whatever they say to you, just keep saying you want a lawyer. Remember that."

She was gripping the bedstead again, so that she could feel the strain in her arms. She said, "It's not true that this is over. Or that I'm in the clear. Those were just things we said last night."

"No," Paul said urgently, "it *is* true. They may suspect

you. They may find some evidence against you, even. But that's a long way from having grounds to arrest you. Megan, the way the system works—it's not the cops doing brilliant detective work, or the lawyers making great speeches to the jury. It's not like TV. It's like—it's like kindergarten. Teacher catches one kid, and he blames it all on somebody else. That's how they get convictions. Without the thief they'll never be able to put together a case against you that will hold up. The only way they can get you now is if you crack. And you won't crack."

Megan flinched. "He said something like that to me once."

"Who?"

"Steve. The thief. The killer. He told me that, too."

"Don't think about him anymore. He's gone. He's out of our lives."

"I don't know. I think I let him too deep into our lives. I told him too much. And he—somehow, he knows more than I told him. He even knew about you. He told me you wouldn't turn me in. He said that because it was murder you'd keep quiet. Until they really leaned on you."

Paul was very still. "What do you mean by that?"

"I have to go now. And I don't want you to call me. Or come see me. Not today. Not for a while. It's dangerous. And we have to be careful."

"You think that I—"

"They have to get somebody to turn me in. That's what you said. They can't get Steve now. So there's only you."

She could not see his face in the darkness. But he dropped his head and shook it a little, as if he were in pain and dizzy, as if she had struck him a physical blow. She hated to go on. "If they find out about you they've got a lot to threaten you with. They can take away your license. They can put you in jail."

"Megan, I won't betray you. No matter what."

"Don't say that. You don't know what you're saying."

"I know the way the system works. I know the tricks. They'll never get me to—"

"You don't know what being afraid is like. Being as scared as I was yesterday. I've been trying to think how to tell you, but there aren't any words. It's everything you take for granted and count on being gone. The worst thing is how you long for safety. You—you *desire* it, the way you've never desired anything. You know the fear is destroying you, just as cold or hunger would. And you want safety the way you'd want warmth or food. You'll do anything to be safe. Paul, listen to me. I'm telling you something that I know. I wanted to be safe so bad that I went down and found that—that murderer and helped him get away. If I could be made to do that, you could be made to turn me in."

"No. Never. I'll stand up for you no matter what."

The words called up a faint echo in her mind. She had to reach far back into the past, to the day she had been fired, and had said to Paul, I would have stood up for you. She had forgotten all about that. She realized that the words had never been out of his mind since she spoke them. She said, "Whatever you owed me, you've paid back. You've done too much for me already. I can't ask any more of you."

"It's got nothing to do with owing. I love you. I won't betray you."

"Oh, don't say that. You don't know what they can do to you. I'm sorry for leading you into this. You've got to keep away from me." She felt too miserable to say anything more. She turned and left the room, shutting the door behind her.

She heard it open, heard his step on the stair, his voice call her name, but she did not turn.

The day was gray and cold, and the wind from the sea was strong enough to rock her car on the more exposed sections of the turnpike. She stayed in the right-hand lane, and when she got off at Stamford, drove slowly through the quiet streets. There was no hurry about getting home. The light at her corner changed to red as she approached it, and she stopped. But her right-turn blinker was on, and the driver behind her hooted impatiently, urging her out of his way. She was looking left for oncoming traffic, so she was already around the corner before she turned her head and saw that her street was filled with police.

There were blue cars everywhere, there was an army of men in black leather jackets. She stepped on the brake. The engine died because she hadn't stepped on the clutch. The car behind her honked again. Faces beneath shiny visors were turning toward her now. She shut her eyes and bowed over the wheel.

The door was pulled open and the wind rushed in. She looked up at a jowly, mustached face. The man said, "See your license, please," and he made her take it out of her wallet, just the way they did when they stopped you for a speeding ticket. She fumbled for a long time, and once she gave it to him he hardly seemed to glance at it before ordering her out of the car. But of course they knew who she was.

There were a lot of men coming toward her as she straightened up, hurrying so that their clubs swung from their belts. She couldn't look at anyone's face. Beyond, there were more of them, coming out of her home. There were so many of them.

She dropped her head. She could tell they were all around her. A hand grasped her arm, but did not urge her forward. They didn't seem to know what to do with her. They were talking, but she did not try to make out the words. She was withdrawing into herself. All her strength was needed to keep her standing up. Finally they started moving. Someone had taken her other arm by now.

There was a car in front of her. The back door was opened and she was put into it. The door closed. She raised her head and looked at the steel cage between the seats. She did not look beyond it. The other doors were opened, and a man got in beside her. He wore an ordinary checked jacket, not a uniform, but there was a badge hanging from his breast pocket. Another man got in the front seat. She did not look at him, but she felt the car settle under his weight.

Megan was numb and weak. She did not feel the fear she had come to know so well. Perhaps she would not feel it again, now that what she had feared was happening.

A card was put in her hands, a long, narrow card like a bookmark, and a pen. The man beside her spoke softly and quickly. "Read this and sign it. And put the date and time where it says."

She looked at the card for a long time before she could make out the first words: "You have the right to remain silent. . . ." It was her Miranda warning. She wondered if their giving her this meant that she was under arrest. She couldn't bear to look at the card. But the man beside her was growing impatient, so she scrawled her name on the bottom. She had to ask them the date and the time. It was hard to get herself to speak, and her voice was almost inaudible. The card was taken from her.

The man in the front seat asked her name and where she lived. She answered, without thinking how pointless the questions were, without thinking about anything. The man's voice was deep, even gentle. He was a black man, middle-aged, and he wore glasses. Megan kept her eyes fixed on him. She didn't want to look at the man beside her; she could sense his avidity.

"Occupation?"

For some reason she was slow to answer, and the other man spoke at once. "Come on, what do you *do*, Megan?" He pronounced it "Meegan." How could he get her name wrong when she had just given it?

"I'm a clerk-typist."

"And before that?"

"I was a paralegal."

She was still looking at the mild black man in front. He was writing on a clipboard. His eyes came up. "When was the last time you saw this guy Scapro?"

Megan stared blankly back. His eyes shifted to his colleague. The man beside her said, "He used another name with you, huh? What was it? What's he known to you by?"

Megan still didn't understand.

"Come on, come on. The guy you went in on the job with. The guy who killed Mrs. Elkin. His name's Steve Scapro, whatever he told you. Now when'd you see him last?"

But Megan had seen that momentary doubt that flickered between the two men. They didn't know everything. It wasn't over yet. She kept silent.

"Come on, Meegan, when'd you last see him?"

They can't even get my name right, Megan said to herself. They don't know who I am. She could still keep it from them. She met the eyes of the black man, the one who was taking down her answers, and put her whole soul into the denial. "I don't know what you're talking about. I don't know anyone called Scapro."

Absurdly, the one beside her asked again, "What's your occupation?"

160

She was now able to think before she answered: she had already told them this, so it was all right to tell them again. "Clerk-typist."

"And where do you work?"

"Kel-Dro Corporation. Jefferson Street in Stamford."

"When did you meet Steve Scapro for the first time?"

Megan kept silent. She felt a warming pulse of anger. Did they think they could make her answer by reflex? Did they think she was too stupid to keep her mouth shut? She was beginning to remember things now: It's hard not to answer. For some reason it's easier to lie than to keep silent. That was something Paul had said. All the rest that Paul had said came rushing into her mind.

She told the man with the clipboard, "I want a lawyer. I'm not answering any more questions without a lawyer."

She saw his lips compress, saw him look at his partner. Each time they looked at one another she felt stronger.

"You're not doing yourself any good this way, Meegan. Where did you meet this guy Scapro for the first time? Down in the city?" He was raising his voice now, and it seemed to her that both of them were smaller and farther away. She could feel space around her. Her mind reached forward to a time when these men would go away for a while and leave her with an ally.

She said again, "I want a lawyer."

The detective beside her swore, in a rush of coffee-scented breath. Then both of them got out of the car. The springs rebounded and it shook as the doors slammed. Megan looked through the cage: another car was pulling up, a small, bright-colored car that would not belong to the police. It came to a stop. Stephanie Feltch checked her makeup in the driving mirror and got out.

She was wearing a blue Yale sweatshirt, jeans, and running shoes that made her easy, swinging gait more pronounced. She had a cup of coffee in hand. The detectives and a couple of the uniformed men gathered around her and began to talk. Sometimes she looked at whoever was speaking, sometimes she seemed interested only in her coffee. Then she began to talk, and the cops did not like what she said. One or another would back away, shaking his head, then come forward with an angry reply. Megan could not tell what anyone was saying, but she could hear the tone of voice and see the misted breath. Beyond the tight, contentious knot, the other cops were getting back into their cars, talking on the radio and drinking coffee. Traffic kept trickling through the street. There was an old woman in a bathrobe standing on the doorstep of the house across the street. She peered in at Megan. She did not look away when their eyes met. It was Megan who looked away.

The group broke up. Engines coughed into life and cars began to pull out. Stephanie Feltch walked over and got in beside Megan, leaving the door ajar. Her skin was glowing and her splendid dark eyes were clear. She looked as if she had been doing something pleasant and relaxing when the call came, and she would return to it when this was over. She had gotten rid of her cup and now held a pack of cigarettes, which she offered to Megan.

"I don't smoke."

"Well, hang on to that at least." She put the cigarettes away without taking one herself. "Seems like everybody who's in jail smokes all the time. It's really disgusting."

Megan said, "I'm not going to jail."

"No. Not right now, anyway. Right now you're not even going to the station for questioning. You said the magic words and made the cops disappear. For a little while, anyway. You played it tough and smart. Like a real pro. I'd almost think you were expecting this." Stephanie Feltch lowered her head to bring her eyes to bear on Megan. "You were, weren't you? I mean, you're not really surprised that this terrible thing is happening to you. You knew you wouldn't get away with it."

"I haven't done anything. I wouldn't talk to the police, and I won't talk to you."

"Right. If you'll notice, I'm talking to you. Maybe I shouldn't, but things have gotten kind of screwed up here today, and it can't do any harm. It may do some good. See, you and I are going to know each other for a long time. We'll think about each other for the rest of our lives. But this is probably the only time we'll ever really talk." She looked out through the grille. All the police cars had gone now, and a pair of uniformed men stood hunched over in the lee of a building. "We better give these guys their car back. Come on."

She got out. Megan pulled the lever at her side, but it didn't work. She had to wait for Stephanie Feltch to come around and open the door for her. They went into the apartment building and up the stairs. Her door was standing ajar. When she saw that, Megan stopped. Stephanie Feltch went in and sat down on the couch.

"Hey, it's your place. Come in. Take a look around."

The living room was not so bad. The carpets were rumpled, the cabinet drawers pulled out, a few pieces of furniture askew. Then she looked into the kitchen. The cupboards stood open and empty, and all the dishes and cans and boxes were on the counters and the floor. In the sink was a gray mound. She stared at it for a moment before realizing that they had dumped out her flour and coffee canisters. She turned away to the bedroom. Her bed had been stripped, the mattress lifted from the box spring. The trash can had been upended. Her clothes lay in heaps on the floor. She looked down at her feet, and saw the contents of her desk drawers—checking-account statements, old letters from her parents and sister, an article about the hazards of IUD's that she had clipped from a magazine, a poem she had liked and copied out longhand. Instinctively, foolishly, she bent and turned the poem face-down. At least there had been no letters from Paul for them to find.

The thought made her feel better. There had been nothing about Paul for them to find; there had been nothing at all for them to find. She had cleaned the place thoroughly last night. There were no papers from the firm, there was nothing Steve had touched. What they had done to her they had done in vain.

With slow steps she went back into the living room, where the damage wasn't so bad. Stephanie Feltch was still sitting on the couch. Megan went to the window, turning her back on her.

"They had no right to do this."

"You're referring to the probable-cause issue? There will be a hearing to determine that. I'll go so far as to say that your lawyer will have a case. Of course, it'll be my job to argue that they did have a right."

"Do you like your job?"

"At some times more than others. I'm just one cog in the

system, and I think that on the whole we're better off with the system than we'd be without it. That's what I tell myself. When it doesn't work, I think that in a couple of years I'll get myself a plush job doing civil litigation, where nobody goes to prison. Of course some of the people I sent to prison will still be there. You could be there for twenty-five years."

"I'm not going to prison. I've done nothing."

Stephanie Feltch waited a moment, then went on. "We were talking about the cops. They figured they were on a roll. They were doing a canvass early this morning, waking up your neighbors, showing Scapro's mug shot. No luck. Finally somebody had the bright idea of asking about the car. That's something the NYPD passed on. Seems Scapro has a girlfriend, and the girlfriend has a car. Distinctive car. A yellow Fiat Spyder with rust spots and a noisy engine."

Megan felt the muscles in her back stiffening. She gripped the window ledge and said nothing.

"Somebody remembered the car. On Monday it was parked here for about half an hour. Right near dinnertime, when the man of the house was expected home. Apparently people in this neighborhood feel strongly about their parking turf, and they get irritated about strange cars with New York plates taking up space in front of their house. When our informant noticed there was a guy sitting in the car, she kept an eye on it." The sound of Stephanie's voice changed as she leaned forward. "So she saw you, when you came along and the guy honked and you got in the car. Didn't know your name, but gave us a good description. Apparently you walk a lot, and people in this neighborhood think that's pretty weird, too."

Megan stepped back from the window. But she did not want to turn and face the prosecutor. She stayed where she was, looking down.

"So the cops came over here. Knocked on your door. When you didn't answer, they came in anyway. And once they were in—"

"They had no right," Megan murmured.

"Like I say, some judge will have to rule on that." Stephanie Feltch got up from the sofa and came to stand behind her. "Don't let this newfound infatuation with your constitutional rights carry you away, Megan. You've lost your old life.

164

It ended this morning. Get yourself that lawyer you keep talking about, quick. You and he are going to be spending a lot of time at the station. And if you want to break the news to anybody before the media get hold of it, better move fast. And don't be late with the rent, because your landlord may start looking for excuses to boot you out. If he lets you stay, I wouldn't try borrowing a cup of sugar from the neighbors. Next week the cops will be at your office, asking about you. See, Megan, they know it's you. Now they're trying to get grounds for me to make out a warrant for your arrest. By the time I do, it'll almost be a relief for you."

Down in the street a car was going slowly past, a big, plain car, without chrome or white sidewalls, but with a spotlight on the fender. Megan said, "Are they going to watch me, too? Follow me?"

Stephanie Feltch ignored the question. "They'll keep on canvassing. And maybe they'll turn up somebody who saw something else. You'll know what there is for them to find. Me, I'm counting on your pal Scapro."

Listlessly Megan repeated, "I don't know anybody named Scapro."

The prosecutor went on as if she hadn't spoken. "Scapro has a yellow sheet longer than you'd believe possible for a guy who's still a month away from his twenty-first birthday. He's got charges against him pending in three counties right now. He's what my colleagues in the police department refer to as an asshole. Staying out of trouble is something he doesn't know how to do. He'll get picked up for something, sooner or later. Then he'll get shipped back here, and I'll offer him a deal. Or he'll offer me one, probably. He knows the ropes. He'll be dying to rat you out, Megan. Don't doubt that."

Megan swung around to face her. "Only you haven't got him yet, have you?" Stephanie Feltch's brow furrowed and she looked at Megan narrowly. Too late Megan realized she should not have said this. She was not thinking so clearly any more.

"That's true. They haven't got him yet." Stephanie was looking troubled now. She was not as glib as before. "One of the cops told me something. Out on the street just now. They've been talking to people at Goldman Lasch. And they picked up this rumor about you. I didn't like hearing about it. I hope it has no bearing on the case. But I sure wish I knew why you weren't home when the cops came calling at dawn. And I sure wish I hadn't been talking shop with Paul yester—"

"Leave Paul alone!" Megan cried out. "He's got nothing to do with this. He told me nothing. I haven't seen him in weeks. Not for weeks."

"Oh, I want to. I'd hate to think that either Paul or I could be that stupid. I'm just as glad not to know. See, there are a lot of things about this case that I don't know. I don't know what you're like. Maybe I'll find out you're a cold, vicious person, and I'll be able to look back on making a deal with Scapro to let him off lightly and send you to prison for most of the rest of your life as a real accomplishment. Something to be proud of. But I don't think I'll have any such luck."

Stephanie Feltch's eyes were so beautiful that it would be easy to imagine there was genuine compassion in them. Megan turned away from her. "You'll do your job anyway. Won't you?"

"Yes. But I'm picky this time. I don't want to cut any deals with fucking Scapro. I want him in a courtroom. I want a jury to say he's guilty, and a judge to hit him over the wall. Megan, if you've got any kind of line on him, if you have any idea where he's gone, tell me. Help me get him. Testify against him. You'll only be charged as accomplice to burglary, and I'll give you the lowest rec I can. I'm not saying you'll walk. But you'll go to the bucket, not the joint. And it'll be for months, not years."

Megan was backing away, shaking her head. Stephanie Feltch stared at her. "I'm trying to help you. Don't you understand?"

"Oh, I understand. I understand how you work. It's simple. If you get Scapro you make him turn on me. If you've got me you try to make me turn on him. You'll say anything. You'll tell any lie you have to. Just so you can scare somebody into betraying somebody else, it's all the same to you."

"Betray. *Betray?*" Stephanie brayed the word out scornfully. Her face flushed red with anger. "My God. What do you think is going on here? Who do you think this guy Scapro is?" She advanced on Megan. "Maybe I'd better tell you what happened in the house that night."

"No. I'm not going to believe you. I won't talk to you

without a lawyer." Her back hit the wall and she could go no further. Stephanie moved even closer.

"I've seen her bedroom. There's a lot of blood in that room but the biggest stain is by the door. She must have heard a noise and she was going to see what it was. Maybe she was so sleepy she thought the children were in the house, and it was one of them. Before she got to the door it opened and Scapro came at her. We don't know how long she lay there after he finished with her. It's a big bloodstain, but she would have been bleeding a lot. Four knife wounds in the shoulder and breast. Only all of them missed the heart. She was still alive. She managed to get to the French windows across the room. Get through them to the balcony. Maybe she thought she was escaping, getting out of the house. If she could still think at all. When she got to the rail and couldn't go any farther she screamed. That we're sure about. People heard that scream two, three houses away. Only Scapro heard it too. He wasn't gone yet. He came back and tore her throat out."

Megan turned away, into the corner. She sank to her knees and hunched over, shut her eyes and covered her face with her hands. But that only made what she was seeing more vivid and unbearable. It was not what Stephanie Feltch had described. It was Barbara Elkin as Megan had seen her, the one time she had seen her. Barbara Elkin with her tanned, lined face and bright blue eyes, her graying blond hair in a pigtail. Barbara Elkin who was dead because of her.

"Think about it, Megan. Get yourself that lawyer. You don't have much time."

By the time she was able to raise her head a little, Stephanie Feltch had gone. She was all alone.

2

It was raining. She looked up to see that the window was streaked and spattered. The wind was howling and driving the rain against it. The storm must have been going on for some time, but she had not noticed when it began. She was still sitting on the floor in the corner of the dim room, and she did not move until she heard the footfalls through the thin wall. Someone was coming up the stairs. She slid back, wedged herself deeper into the angle where the walls met. She stared at the door. It was standing ajar.

Paul pushed it open. He glanced around the disordered room and then saw her. He started toward her. She flung up her hand, to keep him back, to block him from her sight. "No! Don't get near me. You've got to stay away from me."

Paul came to stand over her. He took the outstretched hand.

"Stay away! They're out there watching. They've seen you. Stay away from me."

She tried to snatch her hand free, but Paul held onto it. He did not speak a word or seem to hear her. He braced his legs and pulled and she had to scramble to her feet. He caught her to him.

"Go away. Don't you understand? There's a car out front. They're watching."

He held her close and whispered, "They may be listening too. They may have planted something. Come on."

Still gripping her hand, he led her through the ransacked

kitchen and out onto the fire escape. The rain was beating against the iron stairs and the wall of the building. She flinched as the wind blew the freezing drops into her face. Paul took off his coat and draped it over her shoulders.

"Did they have a warrant for this? Did they show you a court order?"

"There's a car out front—"

"Then they've already seen me. There's nothing to be done about that. What happened here? Did they take you to the station? Interrogate you? What did you tell them?"

She shook her head.

"Megan, try to pull yourself together. It's important that—"

"No. It doesn't matter," she murmured. She did not care about police and prosecutors and what they could do to her. It had not been the law that she feared. Something great and heavy had been poised to fall upon her, and with all her schemes and struggles she had not been able to get out of its cold black shadow. It was not the law, it was just a simple fact. Barbara Elkin was dead because of her.

"My God, Megan—what did they do to you?"

"Oh, Paul, go away. Leave me."

"No. Tell me what they did to you."

She was trying to take off his coat but he gripped her hands and held them still. He wasn't going and she would have to talk. She said, "I've been thinking about Barbara Elkin."

She could feel his steady gaze on her but could not meet it, could not get her head up.

"You never meant her any harm."

"No. That's not true. I kept saying that. I kept trying to put it in the way, but it's not true. I meant her harm. I meant to steal things from her." Now that she had started, her thoughts poured out of her. It was some slight relief from the pain that filled her mind. "I was so angry at her for what she did to me. But that was only one moment in her life, one bad moment when she was upset about the will, scared about what Brian might do—there was so much more to her that I didn't know about. She was loved and needed by a lot of people. She's going to be missed for a long time. Her children—"

"Megan, what did they do to you?"

"Stephanie Feltch told me how she died."

169

"Stephanie was there? Stephanie worked on you too?"

"She told me Mrs. Elkin was in bed, and she must have heard a noise—"

"Megan, stop."

But she could not stop now. She had to say it all. Paul went away from her; he turned his back and leaned on the railing, staring out into the rain. Still she went on until it was finished.

Paul turned. His face was white, but he kept his voice even. "You can't believe anything a prosecutor says when she's working on you. She's trying to break you, so she makes it sound as bad as she can."

"It's much worse than I thought. Much worse than what Scapro told me." She had realized this as she repeated what Stephanie Feltch had said. She dug deeper into her memory. "He said he was in the hall. He had the knife because he was cutting a painting out of the frame. She came on him and he panicked. He struck at her and ran. He didn't say anything about going back."

"That fits. That at least makes sense. But what Stephanie's saying—"

"Why should I not believe her? Why should I believe Scapro? I know what he is. But I've believed everything he's told me, because I was in it with him. He convinced me I was in it with him."

"What Stephanie says is crazy. It wouldn't make sense unless he—unless he went looking for Barb. But he didn't even know she was there. He thought the house was empty. That was why you chose Thanksgiving night. Because you thought the house would be empty."

"No. That's not how it was. I said Wednesday night. It was agreed to go on Wednesday. But then at the last moment the fence changed it. No—that's not right either. Scapro told me the fence had changed it to Thanksgiving night."

"Does that matter? You thought the house would be empty on Thanksgiving too. And it would have been if Barb hadn't changed her plans."

Megan held up a hand to stop him. Her thoughts were so slow and fumbling. "Scapro told me the fence had changed his plan. And Mrs. Elkin had changed her plan . . ."

"You didn't know that."

"No. I didn't know. So I accepted that it was just—just bad luck that she was there and she died. Because if it was bad luck, it couldn't be anyone's fault. It couldn't be my fault."

"How could it be anything but bad luck? The thief had no connection to the Elkins but you. You didn't know, so he didn't know. He thought the house was empty. Otherwise he would never have gone in. He just went there to rob the house. Not to—to kill Barb Elkin."

A gasping sob was torn from Megan. She felt as if all the breath had been knocked out of her. She grabbed for the railing. But her legs did not buckle, and soon she found that she could breathe again. There was only the one hard jolt. It was like the moment when a dream she'd believed in had gone on too long and stretched too thin, and her mind rejected it. Then she would wake with a start and blink about her at the unfamiliar outlines of things that were real.

She saw it all whole now. She saw how small a part she had played in it. She saw how small she had been. "Oh, Paul, he did. Scapro went there to kill her. It wasn't a robbery at all any more. He went there on Thanksgiving night so she would be there and he could kill her."

Paul was silent, staring at her.

"I told him all about the Elkins, and he saw that he could get much more from her death than he'd ever get from a robbery. I was trying to talk him out of the robbery because I was afraid of you. He made me tell him about you. He made me tell him about the Elkins. And he saw how much her murder was worth."

"Her murder was worth—?"

"How much is Brian Elkin going to get now?"

Paul flinched with the shock of it. All was so clear and fixed in her own mind that she had not realized how hard it would hit him. She repeated, "How much does he get?"

It was a long moment before he answered, and when he did his thoughts seemed far from the dry, inevitable words. "The trusts terminate with Barb's death. The estate will be divided up equally among issue. So Brian gets a fourth."

"That will be a lot."

"Yes. Over a million." He shook his head slightly. "But how do you know? How do you know that Brian—"

"Because I was told. Scapro went straight to the city and found Brian Elkin and talked him into it. I was told that last night, only I didn't hear. Scapro's girlfriend said that he wasn't working with me. He had a deal going with a guy. She even described Brian. She called him the Soho guy with pink sunglasses. I should have remembered where Brian lives. I sent him enough letters from the firm. I should have remembered those tinted glasses he wore."

"I haven't talked to him since . . ." Paul was still lost in his own thoughts. "I've been putting him off, avoiding him the way I always did. He was bitter and troublesome, and he was always so sorry for himself that there was nothing left for anyone else to do. It was a lot easier to make fun of him than—" Paul broke off, and his eyes narrowed. "He was supposed to be there on Thanksgiving. At his uncle's. He's invited every year and he never comes. But this year Barb made his uncle try especially hard. She wanted to patch things up. She always wanted to get along with him."

"That was what he really hated," Megan said. She was looking through the open door into the kitchen. She thought of the night when Brian Elkin had come to claim his share of her disaster. He had sat at that table and told her all about his fortune that was dangled before him and denied him, of the young family who over many happy years would swallow it all up and leave him with nothing. Brian had disgusted her, and she had thrown him out before he was finished indulging his rancor.

What a revenge he had almost taken of her for that slight. She said aloud, "If Scapro hadn't botched the job—if Barb Elkin hadn't screamed, he would have gotten away clean. I'd never have seen him again. I'd never have known how he and Brian used me. And for the rest of my life I would have felt the way I've felt these last two days. With the guilt slowly tearing me up, not knowing there was anything I could do about it."

Paul raised his head, came out of his reverie. He looked at her with sadness. "Megan, there is nothing you can do about it."

"Yes. There is something I can try. I've got to try."

"You can't go to the police with this. Or to Stephanie. You have nothing they can use on Brian. You have no proof. But once you've started talking to them they've got you. If they can't make the felony murder charge stick they can surely get you for accomplice to burglary. Your only chance of getting off is to keep silent, hope their case against you breaks down."

"Oh, Paul, I'm not going to get off." She reached out to touch his face. "That's just foolishness. Let that go. You're even more scared for me than I am, and you're not thinking straight. I've done something bad, and I'll have to pay for it."

"No. That's not true. You didn't know what you were doing. They used you."

"They couldn't have done it without me. Now I'm the only one who can bring out the truth. So I have to do it."

"Truth is no use to the cops, or to Stephanie. They need evidence."

"Then maybe I can bring them a witness. Scapro's girl-friend. She saw them together. She didn't know what they were doing, but she can identify Brian Elkin. Can Stephanie do anything with that?"

He thought a moment. "Stephanie could do a lot with that. If this girl could be made to talk. But—"

"Scapro's gone now. What she says can't hurt him. I think she may be willing to help me, but only if I ask her."

Paul stared wildly at her. "For God's sake, Meg. You're not going down there. You can't make somebody like that talk. Leave it to the police. They know how to put on the pressure."

"Marla knows all about pressure, too. She hardly knows anything else. The only way she might help is if I ask her. I've got to try it. I've got to go now."

"What about that car out there? If you leave they'll follow. If you cross the state line they'll arrest you. They're just waiting for you to make a stupid mistake like this so they can lock you up. So forget it. What you've got to do is—"

"Paul, don't tell me what to do. I know what to do."

He stopped short and turned a little away from her. But Megan stepped up to him and gripped both his arms and looked into his face. "I know what to do," she repeated. "Don't you see? I've stopped feeling bad."

He spoke so softly that she could hardly hear him over the

racket of the rain. "What you said before—you were right. I'm pretty damned scared for you. This sounds crazy."

"No, there's a chance."

"But what about that cop out there?"

"I'm going to have to get away from them for a while."

"How?"

She drew in a breath. "I've been thinking about that, and all I can think of is—you'll have to drive me to town. I'll try to slip out of the car without being seen. So that the cop keeps on following you."

She made herself stop there. There was no point in warning him of what would happen when the police caught up with him. He would know better than she. She wanted to say she was sorry, too, but that would be absurd. What she was asking was too great.

Paul looked past her, out into the rain. He had his impassive lawyer's face on, and she had never been more uncertain of what was going on in his mind. After a moment he dug in his pocket and she heard the jingle of his keys.

"I can't think of any better way to do it," he said. "Let's go."

The cold rain bit at her ears and neck as she followed Paul out the door. She bent her head and kept it down, not wanting to see the unmarked car. It was so dark that she thought the November dusk was closing in already. But the clock on the dashboard said quarter to one.

Paul started the engine. Taking his glasses out of his pocket, he put them on. If he was not calm, he certainly looked it. Then he put the car in gear and drove to the the end of the street. The signal was red. They waited. She saw Paul glance in the mirror, and there was a bar of reflected light across his face: the headlights of the car behind. The signal changed and he pulled away.

"He's staying right on my bumper. He wants us to know he's there. I guess the idea is to hassle you, keep the pressure on."

"That's going to make it tougher to—"

"Yeah."

The windshield wipers swished and flopped at their fastest setting, but even so they could just keep the glass clear. The raindrops were making a fusillade on the top of the car. The taillights of cars ahead cast long blurred streaks in the gleaming pavement. The streetlamps had come on; they glowed feebly against the dirty gray sky. Cars threw up fans of water from deep puddles at the curb. Traffic began to clot up as they neared the downtown mall. For other people this was Saturday after Thanksgiving, a day for Christmas shopping. In another block they were walled in and immobile. She saw Paul glance in the mirror and knew that the police car was still right behind them.

"We've got to get you near the station," he said. "And then we've got to get out of this guy's sight for a second."

"If you could get a little ahead of him—turn a corner and I could jump out . . ."

"He's too close. I can't try any tricks on him. He probably knows the tricks and I don't. If he figures we're trying to pull something on him, he won't fool around with us. We've got to do it without making him suspicious. I—"

He stopped speaking and she saw, just from the set of his shoulders, that now he had an idea. He turned in his seat, and with gestures negotiated his way into the left-turn lane. The signal changed, and they swung into the long, straight street that ran between the concrete flank of the elevated turnpike and the garage entrances of the big office buildings. The street led right to the station, and since the buildings were closed there was little traffic. Megan did not understand what he was doing, until he switched on his blinker, slowed, and turned into the entrance of the Goldman Lasch building. He stopped in front of the brightly striped crossbar. The guard in the booth leaned forward to squint at the windshield sticker, then raised the bar. Paul waved and pulled through.

"Has he stopped him?"

Megan swiveled round in her seat. "Yes. They're talking."

The scene slid from her view behind a concrete pier. Paul turned sharply and they plunged down a ramp. When they reached the lower level he stepped on the gas and they sped through the vacant cavern. "I'll try to leave the car and get upstairs before he catches up. The guy may not know what we've pulled. You may have time. But don't count on it. If he sees me alone all I can do is start talking. I'll bullshit him like crazy, but it won't last long. They'll start looking for you. They may check the trains. Get off at the first stop in the Bronx. Switch to the subway."

"I will," she said. "You're wonderful, Paul, I love you."

With an echoing squeak of tires he brought the car to a stop near the stairs. "Go!"

Megan jumped from the car. It was moving again even as she swung the door shut. She ran up the stairs and out the door to the rainswept sidewalk. It had happened so fast; only now did she realize that at the last instant Paul had gripped her hand.

$$3$$

Megan came up the steps from the subway and stood looking anxiously around her. She'd had to guess at the stop, and at first she was not sure she had guessed right. The area looked different in the day. But when she came to the first intersection, she saw the big, bright windows of the laundromat. She walked on until she came to the narrow alley behind the row of grim apartment buildings. She made the long climb up the fire escape and knocked on the door at the top.

There was a moment when she held her breath, thinking the girl was not home, but then she heard the click and clatter of bolts being undone. The door slid open a crack and Marla looked out. A shudder of surprise passed over her face, then left it as hard and blank as it had been before.

"What do you want? He's *gone*, you ought to know that."

"I know."

"I took him to a bus terminal. Way the hell over in Jersey, where there wouldn't be cops hanging around. He's gone, understand? I mean, you saw us leave."

"I know he's gone. I came to talk to you, Marla."

"We got nothing to talk about, lady." She shut her eyes in vehemence.

"My name is Megan Lofting."

"I don't want to know your name." She jerked her head back and the door began to close.

"No!" Megan cried out. She braced her hand against the door. The girl went on pushing, so Megan pushed harder. The door flew open. Marla resisted no further. She retreated into the room, eyes downcast. With a small, neat movement, she sat down on the floor. Her face was slack, like the face of a trapped and wretched child who retreats deep into her own mind.

Megan stepped in and closed the door. Now she saw the gray mound of powders in the kitchen sink, the counters covered with dishes and glasses. The thin carpet was rolled back from the stained linoleum floor. The cushions were slit, the beaded curtain a glinting heap in the doorway. The light in the room was harsher: she looked up to see that the paper shade had been torn down. Nothing could have been hidden in that shade; it had just been hanging there, prominent and fragile as a balloon, and so the cops had destroyed it.

She said, "They broke a lot more here than they did in my place."

The girl did not look up. She said, "They weren't trying to find nothing. They just did it to impress me."

"How did they get on to you?" The girl did not answer. "Was it your parole officer, like you said last night?"

Marla drew her legs up, wrapped her arms around them. After a while she said, "Yeah. That jerk Larry. He's real tight with the cops. He told 'em about me and Steve. They been working on me for hours. Here. At the station."

"What did you tell them?"

"Only thing I could tell them. I didn't see Steve for months.

177

They come at me all kinds of different ways but they couldn't get me to say anything else."

"I understand," Megan said, and she did. Now that she had been interrogated herself, she knew that when there was no other defense, all you could do was armor yourself in a willed stupidity. She did not think that Marla was stupid at all. She sat down in front of the girl, who peered warily at her over her raised knees. "They'll be back."

"Oh yeah. They were real pissed off when they didn't find drugs or anything, so they could take me away right then. They'll come back. They'll plant some stuff if they have to. I'm on parole. It's no trick getting me back in jail. I'm not like you."

"We're more alike than you think. I've run from them. I have very little time left."

"You running? How come you're not on a bus or something? How come you're here?"

"I came to ask for your help."

The girl's face grew taut with wariness, as if Megan had threatened her. She gripped her knees more tightly. "I can't help you."

Megan leaned closer. "Remember what you said to me last night? You said—"

"I don't remember. A lot's happened since last night."

"You said I didn't have a deal with Steve and you were right. I thought I did, but I was wrong. Steve's deal was with the guy you saw. The Soho guy with pink sunglasses. Remember?"

"No. I don't remember." But the denial was more hesitant this time. Marla still did not know what her lover had gotten himself into, and part of her wanted to know. She bent her head so that Megan could see only the white line of the parting in her lank dark hair. Megan's heart was pounding, but she made herself keep still and wait. At last the girl muttered into her sleeve, "What do you want from me anyway?"

"I want you to come with me. To the state attorney in Stamford. I want you to identify that man."

Marla kept her head down and tightened her embrace of herself. "I can't identify nobody. I don't know what you're talking about."

"You can. You even described him last night. I know who you were talking about."

"That's you saying that. I don't remember anything."

Megan sank back into a sitting position. This time the silence went on and on. But she was going to make Marla break it.

At last the girl burst out, "What are you sitting around for? The cops are coming back here. You want them to find you? You better get out of here."

"I have nowhere else to go," Megan said. "You're the end of the line for me."

Marla's head came up at that. Her face was working. She put her hands to the floor and pushed herself back from Megan. Megan did not move. "I can't help you. I can't even help myself. They're coming to get me and put me in jail and that's it."

"It doesn't have to be that way. The prosecutor is just a lawyer, and lawyers like to make deals. If you've got something they want, they'll deal with you. And you have something they'll want badly. The man you saw—"

"Stop! Just stop talking, will you?"

Megan broke off at once, and sat waiting and watching. Marla's eyes slitted with suspicion. "I know what you're trying to do. You're trying to get me to rat Steve out."

"That's not what I'm asking."

"Yeah, you only want me to identify this other guy. Only once they got me in there, once they got me talking, they can empty me out. You want me to snitch on Steve."

Megan said: "Where is Steve, Marla?"

"Sure. You think I'm gonna tell you?"

"No, I don't. I don't think you know. Did he tell you last night where he was going? Has he gotten in touch with you since?"

"Well, he couldn't. Not when—"

"Not when he knew what was going to happen to you. He was leaving you to the cops, so he figured he'd better leave you empty. So don't worry about ratting Steve out. He didn't give you the choice."

Marla struggled awkwardly to her feet. "I'm not listening to this shit any more. Go away, will you? Just go away."

"I already told you. I have nowhere else to go."

The girl stood stock-still, glaring, her fists clenched at her sides. Then she ran out the door.

It happened so suddenly that for a moment Megan sat where she was, staring out the open doorway at the rain. Then she rose and hurried out. Even through the pelting of the rain, she could hear Marla's footsteps clattering down the fire escape below her. She started to run after her, but caught herself, thinking that if Marla heard pursuing footfalls she would keep on running. Megan descended the steps slowly, softly. When she reached the bottom she stood still.

Marla was striding down the alley, her head bent against the rain. She glanced over her shoulder. She kept on going, but her steps were slower. Finally she stopped and turned. She was so far away Megan could not see her expression, but the girl's body was poised for flight. If Megan so much as moved a hand, she would shy and flee like a wild animal. Megan waited and tried to keep from her mind what would happen if Marla took half a dozen steps and vanished beyond the corner of the building.

But Marla came back. Slowly. Each step was as halting as the first. She reached the narrow shelter of the fire escape, and leaned against the wall quite close to Megan. Megan had run out of arguments. She could only wait.

At last Marla broke the silence. "Listen, if you want me to help you don't say stuff that gets me mad, okay? Like what you said up there. 'Cause you don't know about me and Steve."

"All right. I'm sorry. But will you help me?"

Marla drew in a deep breath, and Megan sensed that even now she had not made up her mind. But then she said: "I only saw 'em together the one time. Few days ago."

"Tuesday. It would have been Tuesday."

"Yeah, okay."

"Where did you see him?"

"Steve called, said pick him up from one of those fancy places in Soho. So I go in, and I see him with this guy at a table. Soon as he sees me, he comes over. He's like—'Go wait in the car.' And I'm like—'But I got a parking space, I don't have to.' And he's like—'Just leave the car with me, get out of here.' He was real—I figured he'd been doing coke. I figured he had something big going, like the guy was a dealer or something. So he takes the keys off me and I don't see him till late at night. I only saw the guy for a minute and I didn't talk to him or anything."

"Would you recognize him if you saw him again?"

Marla hunched her shoulders and tucked her hands beneath her armpits. She was shivering. She hung her head and looked out at the alley for a long moment. She said, "Yeah."

Then there was an unexpected, perfectly simple moment when they looked at one another and smiled. Megan asked, "Will you come back with me? Now?"

"You got a car? They took mine."

"No. We'll have to use the subway and the train."

"Well, okay."

"We'll get your coat."

Marla looked at the stairs as if they were impossibly steep. "I don't want to go back up there."

"All right. I'll get it for you."

She shook her head. "Let's just *go*, okay?" She turned and started walking fast, folding her arms and hunching her thin shoulders. Megan came up beside her. She had on only a shirt and jeans. Megan started to unzip her coat. "Look, I've got a sweater and—" But the girl only shook her head again.

They came out of the alley to the street. For a time they walked without speaking. Then Marla said: "This guy—who is he?"

"His name is Brian Elkin. He's her stepson. If she died a lot of money would come to him. Steve found that out. They got together."

"Steve's never . . . He's not—" The girl was silent for a moment. Then she said, "That guy, that fence, Klausner, he really rips Steve off, every job Steve does for him. And there's a bondsman and a lawyer, and Steve's into them so deep he'll never get them paid off. There's a lot of people leaning on him. He gets real mad sometimes." She relapsed into her thoughts for a few steps. "It was a lot of money, huh?"

"Yes. I don't know how much Elkin paid him, but Elkin wasn't poor before except in his own eyes, and now he'll be rich. But that wasn't the main thing. The main thing was that he hated his stepmother. Somehow Steve knew that. Knew he'd agree to have her killed."

After another pause Marla said, "Steve had a stepfather. Or he wouldn't call him that. Just the guy who moved in on his mom after his dad split. He used to say—he said how he'd hear 'em in the bedroom, and he was too small to know what they were doing but he didn't like it, and he'd start screaming. The guy would come out and like beat the shit out of him. His mom just stayed in bed." She glanced at Megan. "Steve would tell that story like it was all a big joke on him."

"I don't understand."

"I mean there's things Steve never got a chance to learn. He doesn't know—he doesn't know what other people are."

Poor girl, Megan thought. In her mind no one else's suffering counted as much as Steve's, not even her own. Megan kept silent: she must say nothing that would break her fragile contract with Marla.

"He doesn't know what he's getting into," she went on. "He doesn't think. He's not dumb. I'm not saying that. He's too smart, that's what it is. He gets these ideas, he works out these plans, only he doesn't know what other people are. He thinks he can push 'em around like pushing buttons. Like it's some video game or something. He doesn't feel anything when they get hurt. He doesn't know they can hurt him back."

She fell silent again. But her thoughts slowed her step despite the wind and rain. The storm was growing worse. The traffic signals suspended over the intersection were swaying in the wind. Things clattered and thumped in the dimness. The sidewalks were almost deserted. The two women kept to the lee of the buildings, and away from the curbs and the drenching plumes of water thrown up by passing cars. They didn't talk any more. Megan's thoughts were growing wayward, as they always did when she was worn out. It would be colder when they got to Stamford, she thought. It would be snowing there. She wondered where Paul was at this moment, and what was happening to him. She worried over him and longed for him.

It was a relief to get into the shelter of underground, even into the sickly fluorescent light and the girders and concrete of the subway, the echoing racket and shuffle and babble. Megan bought tokens and they descended down steep stairs and long dank passageways lined with ravaged advertisements to the platform for Manhattan-bound trains. It was confusing, sorting out the tangle of signs, but Marla offered no help. She kept falling behind, and Megan would have to stop and wait for her.

When they reached the platform it was nearly empty. They had just missed a train, and would have to wait for the next. There was space on the benches, but neither of them sat down. Megan leaned against a girder, where she could see down the tunnel. Marla paced aimlessly, her arms folded and head down. Megan longed for the train to come.

At last there was the building, echoing rumble. She straightened up and looked down the tunnel for the lights. But then the sound changed. It was a different train, coming in to a platform above them. Megan turned back, and caught Marla looking at her. There was something in the girl's eyes that gave her a cold stab of alarm. She had to fight the instinct to reach out and grab her arm.

"I'm—I'm just going up for some cigarettes, okay?"

The foolish, desperate lie made Megan wince. The girl had been about to slip away from her. "Oh, Marla. Please. You said you'd help me."

"I'm sorry. I got to think. I'm sorry." She was falling back, step by step, and yet she kept her eyes on Megan's.

"Stay with me and we can get out of this mess. I thought you understood. We can help each other."

"Get out of it?" the girl cried. "You don't even know what's going on. You don't know."

"Steve," Megan said. "He didn't get away. He's here."

Marla spun and ran.

Megan did not hesitate, did not think. She went after her. But the girl was very quick and had opened a gap between them before she took a step. The platform was crowded now. Megan had to keep slowing up, dodging around people. A man looking up the tracks wandered obliviously into her path. She checked at the last moment and her foot slipped. When she got her balance and looked for Marla, she could not see her.

A flicker of movement from the stairway caught her eye—

a gang of boys laughing, craning their heads up the stairs. Marla had just gone past them. Megan ran for the steps. One of the boys got in front of her and made a joke of blocking her, side-stepping with her. It took Megan a second to get free. Their laughter came ringing up the stairs behind her.

At the top was only an intermediate level—dim, empty space between the track platforms. She did not pause but ran for the next staircase. When she reached the top she saw that the narrow strip of concrete before her teemed with people. A train stood on the track, all its doors open, and people were pouring out, going in all directions. She had to slow to a jog, then to a walk, peering, craning around the huddled shapes of raincoated shoulders and hats, trying to catch a glimpse of Marla down the platform. At last she reached the exit stairs, and started up them toward the street. Clinging to the wall she managed to break free of the worst of the crowd. At the top she paused. She could see far down a long narrow passageway, and she could not see Marla. The girl could not have gotten that far ahead of her. She wasn't going back to the street, back to her apartment, at all. Megan had already passed her—passed within yards of her. She had gotten on the train below.

Megan swung round and bumped heavily into a man who was trying to get by her. He staggered back with a curse, and she stumbled down the stairs. Going down it was easier to force her way through the crowd. She heard her voice calling out apologies and pleas.

When she got to the bottom the train was still there, far down the platform. Its doors were open but the flow of people through them had ceased. There was room to run now, and she ran flat-out.

She looked for a figure leaning out a window—for the conductor who would see her and might hold the train for her. She would shout, she would beg him. But she saw no one. He must have turned away, to the controls that operated the doors.

Over her footfalls and her ragged breathing she could hear the ratchety click that the trains made when they were standing still. She was that close.

The noise ceased. The doors slid shut.

"No!" Megan cried aloud.

She was running level with the last car. Faces stared out

at her. She dropped into a jog, gasping. The train had not started moving yet. She came up to the coupling. There were barriers, steel gates projecting from the ends of the cars. But there was a narrow gap between them. She could get through to the doors. She stretched her arm up to reach a handle near the top of the car, and sought a foothold in the gate. She was in midstep when the train started to move.

Her right foot was still on the ground and it was swept out from under her as if someone had grabbed it and pulled. Her body lurched sideways and down. Her foot on the slanting steel bar of the gate began to slide. She gripped the handle with all her might. A pain tore down her arm and shoulder. She thought distinctly that she was going to fall. But her foot slid down into the angle where two bars met and jammed hard. The pressure on her arm eased. Her other hand fumbled and found a hold on the upright of the gate.

The train plunged into the darkness of the tunnel. She realized that, as strong as the force that pulled at her was, the train was moving slowly. Now the wheels sent up a rising howl, a vortex of sound that seemed to pull her down into it. She had to get between the cars before the train began moving any faster.

Blinking against the rushing wind, she slipped her right foot into the gap between the gates. There was a wonderful resting place there, a long, level bar. She got her foot onto it. Now she could let go of one handhold, and grasp another further in. Already the force that pulled on her was less. The other foot was wedged so tightly in the angle of the gate she had to struggle to get it free. She pulled her leg through the gap between the gates.

It was easier now. She was shielded from the momentum of the train. The rounded platforms at the ends of the cars met below her. But the howling still filled her ears, and everything she held was jolting, trying to shake free of her grasp. There was another, inner barrier—a waist-high net of chains. She probed for a foothold but her toes kept bumping uselessly against the chains.

The wheels scraped and screeched against the rails. With a sickening lurch, her body was thrown outward. A gap opened between the platforms under her. The train was going into a turn. She shut her eyes and held on with all her strength. Glare and blackness flickered over her closed eyelids.

At last the pressure let up, as the cars straightened out and shielded her again. She opened her eyes and looked down. There was a headlight housing she could climb onto, a higher handhold she could reach. She raised herself up until her foot could reach the topmost chain of the barrier. She shifted her grip on the handles again and clambered over it.

She dropped down to the platform. It swayed and jolted, and yet to her it felt like solid ground. She let go of the handles. Lifting her head, she could see through the glass into the light and safety of the car. She grasped the door handle and pulled. The door slid open so easily that she lost her balance and pitched forward onto the grimy linoleum floor.

4

A pole was within reach. She grasped it and hauled herself upright. There were a lot of people in the car, and not one of them was looking at her. The faces of the nearer ones vanished under hatbrims and into coat collars. Even if they had not seen any of her antics outside, falling full-length to the floor had been enough. She had joined New York's army of the invisible. No one's eyes met hers as she scanned the car.

Marla wasn't here. But she wouldn't be, of course: she had come up from the other end of the platform, and would have boarded the first car she came to. Megan would find her farther up the train.

When people began to get up, lurching and grabbing for holds, she thought at first that they were moving away from her. But the train was coming into a station. When the doors opened, she moved to the nearest one and peered cautiously out. There was a brief flurry of coming and going, and then the platform was bare. The train moved on. Marla was still aboard.

From handhold to handhold, she made her way the length of the car. Reaching the door, she looked through the glass into the car ahead. No Marla. She would have to keep going. She reached for the door handle, paused to get up her nerve, and stepped across the bucking, clattering gap and through the other door.

It was necessary to make her way through four cars before she found Marla. Pausing at the door and looking through the glass, she saw the girl standing at the opposite end of the next car. Her back was turned; she was staring out the front window at the tunnel rushing past. This was the lead car of the train. It was slowing down as they approached another station, but Marla made no move to get off. She did not even glance at the sign. Clearly she had some distance yet to go.

Megan sank down on the nearest seat. Her heart was pounding. She felt light-headed. She was giddy with adrenaline, with risk and action and coming through unscathed. But she was going to have to calm down now. She cradled her head in her hands, covering her ears to shut out the noise of the train, and tried to gather her scattered thoughts.

It was no use approaching Marla because she would only run again. Her new and tenuous loyalty to Megan had broken under old demands. From what Megan had told her on the street, from all that she knew about her lover, she had decided that Scapro was back in the city. He was ignoring his danger, but she would not. Wherever she was going now, she expected to find him there. Megan could follow her. See where she went. Find a telephone and call the police.

Red drops were falling to the linoleum between her feet. She looked at her hands. They were dirty and covered with scrapes and scratches. The blood was coming from a deep slice across her right palm. She got her gloves out and wiped her face in case she had gotten blood on it. Then she put the gloves on. They were the only bandages she had.

She had not come through unscathed at all. She just hadn't heeded her injuries. Now it seemed that her body was filled with pain. A long fissure of it opened along her shoulder and side when she moved. Her left ankle was throbbing. It was the one that had gotten jammed and twisted in the angle of the gate. That was a bad injury, one that would get worse.

Megan sat back, resting her head against the wall behind her. The train rocked her, and she ached. The pain was sobering. How did she expect to be able to follow Marla, to keep her in sight without being seen? She had no idea how far the girl would make her walk once they left the train. Then she would have to get to a pay phone. And why was she so certain that the police would come promptly at her call? The plan was folly. When the train stopped, she said to herself, she would rise and limp out the doors, and wait for the train going the other way. Begin the long journey home.

But when they pulled into the the next station and the doors in front of her slid open, she leaned forward to check that Marla had not moved, and then leaned back.

I want him in a courtroom, Stephanie Feltch had said that morning. I want the jury to say he's guilty and the judge to hit him over the wall. It was what Megan wanted too. It was why she had run after Marla, why she had jumped the train. She had made her decision the moment she realized that Scapro was not yet beyond her reach. There was no more need to think about it.

Megan bent down to massage her ankle, to move it and test it with her weight. She must try to keep it from stiffening up.

The train came out of the ground and mounted a trestle high over the street. Megan turned to look out. She had no idea where they were anymore; this was like no part of New York City that she had ever seen. Below were tall, narrow wooden houses. Lights glowed cozily from their windows. The train seemed to move more slowly and stop less often. People stood waiting at the doors, doing up their buttons. Night was falling and they were eager to get home. No more passengers were getting on. Her car was emptying fast. When she leaned forward to peer through the glass, she saw that Marla was the only one left in the lead car. The girl swayed and staggered, ignoring the empty seats.

Outside, the lights dwindled. The train descended to run along the ground, and Megan peered out at tumbledown shacks, subsiding into an inlet of black water. It was the ragged edge of the great city: they could not have much farther to go. The land came to an end, but the train ran on. She looked down from the bridge upon long rows of whitecapped waves. Even over the noise of the train she could hear the wind.

They were back on land, now, a marshy island. In the light from the train's windows—the only light—she saw tall reeds flying past. Then there were buildings again and the train began to slow. The platform of a station slid into view. There was nobody waiting on it, and no one got off the train but Marla. Hunched over against the cold, the girl crossed the platform and went down some steps. Megan stepped onto the platform. The doors slid shut, and the train went clattering on its way.

She went down the steps and through the turnstile. Streetlamps shed a wan light on a narrow street between small houses. There were no cars, no people, only Marla, walking quickly away. Megan waited till she rounded a turn and disappeared from sight. Then she went after her.

The rain had left up but the wind was stronger here. Its rush filled Megan's ears and she could hardly keep her head up and her eyes open against it. They were going into it, toward the sea.

She turned a corner onto a straight street. Marla was farther ahead of her now. She was passing a row of sturdy bungalows. Each was enclosed by a chain-link fence. There were stunted trees hung with windblown litter like Christmas tinsel, and here and there laundry snapped and billowed on lines. The blinds of the houses were drawn so that only narrow margins of light showed from within. Cars were parked in front of the houses, like an additional barricade, but there were no cars moving on the street, and no one on the sidewalks. The little village was battened down, keeping its light and warmth to itself. She did not think that Steve Scapro had found his hiding place here. They would be going on a ways.

The girl was getting farther and farther ahead of her. Megan tried to run, but her ankle would not take the weight. She strode on as best she could, lurching at every other step. But she could only watch as the pale speck of the girl's blouse was swallowed up in the darkness. They had come to the end of the streetlamps. She passed a couple of empty husks of cottages. Then the village gave way to the marsh.

She had to slow down even more, because the pavement was broken and buckled. A few more steps and the road was only a rutted, sandy track. On either side the ground sloped away, to stands of reeds and pools of water. The wind howled out of the blackness ahead. Her body hunched and twisted and she could hardly keep her head up. It was like trying to swim against a strong current.

She came to a footbridge. It was only a narrow walkway of boards, but there was a railing to hold onto, and Megan grasped it. Blinking against the wind, she saw that the bridge crossed a sandy reach. There was a brightly lit causeway to her right, but it was far away. In the other direction she could see as far as the straight black line of the sea beneath the cloudy sky. It was several minutes since she had lost sight of Marla, but she must have come this way. Megan stepped onto the bridge. It was so spindly that it rocked a little under her weight. She made her way gingerly across.

She reached the end and stepped onto the ground. There was a stand of tall reeds in front of her. She could hear them clattering in the wind. Peering through smarting eyes she made out the dark shape of a building—a tiny shack, all boarded up. When she took a couple of staggering steps, she saw others farther on. It was a shabby beach colony, long ago shut up and abandoned to the ravages of winter. Now she remembered what Scapro had said last night: I can go to that place of Frank's, that place we went last summer. Marla had told him it wasn't safe, and he had seemed to accede. But he had been deceiving them both, or something had changed his mind. He had come here after all. He was somewhere nearby.

Megan glanced over her shoulder, at the lights of the village in the distance. She would go back now, to pound on the doors of those snug cottages until someone would let her in. She would call the police. She took a step backward, then another. She was so filled with wariness that she could not turn her back on the place where Scapro was. Her hand groped behind her for the railing.

Something coming at her from the darkness. Her heart lurched and she shrank down. But it was Marla. The girl was only steps away from her, running hard. Megan rose and reached out to her. The girl tried to dodge, but Megan grasped her arms. Marla's momentum knocked both of them to the ground.

"What is it?" Megan shouted over the wind. "What did you—?" But the girl was strong with panic. She wriggled free from Megan's hold and got to her feet and ran on. In a second she had vanished among the reeds.

Megan started to run in the direction the girl had come from. She pitched forward with every other step, but she did not feel the pain. Ahead of her down the track through the reeds she saw a light.

It was a flashlight, lying on the ground. Megan bent to pick it up. It was heavy and it threw a brilliant beam that made her narrow her eyes as she shone it around. There were steps leading to a cottage that stood on low posts above the marshy ground. She went up them. The door was shut, the windows boarded. She made her way around the narrow porch, and came to a place where the railing was broken. She shone her light down.

The figure lay half-submerged at the edge of the water. The head turned haltingly, painfully sideways as the man struggled to get breath. She could see the face now. She recognized Brian Elkin.

Megan jumped down from the low platform. A bolt of pain shot up from her ankle and she nearly toppled over. She splashed through the cold water. She could not leave Brian where he was. She shoved the flashlight in her pocket and grasped him under the arms. But the inert body was too heavy.

"Help me," she shouted, "help me, Brian, or you'll die." His arms stirred feebly and his legs thrashed in the water. She was able to haul him clear. When she let go of him he placed his hand flat on the ground and pushed, turning over on his back. He gave a cough that ended in a grunt of pain.

A faint smell came to her from his coat—a smell she knew only from fireworks. He had been shot. Megan got out the flashlight and switched it on. There was a hole torn through his coat, in the middle of his chest. Blood welled out of it. She turned the light on his face. Spittle and blood bubbled on his lips, and his breathing had a terrible liquid sound. His eyes were squeezed shut against the pain and the light. She switched the light off.

"Scapro did this. He shot you." She could not tell if Brian knew who she was, if the sense of her words was even reaching him. But after a moment his head moved in a slight, slow nod.

"Where is he? How long ago—" But then she broke off, realizing that Brian would have no answers for these questions. It did not matter: he could not have been in the water for more than a few minutes, or he would have died. Scapro was running—she hoped that he was running—but he could not be far away. She looked out fearfully into the darkness around them.

Brian was muttering. She leaned toward him and said, "What?"

"Had to try—try for him."

Brian breathed shallowly, painfully for a moment, then went on. "I had no money left. I told him there was no use meeting. Had no more money for him. But he made me come down here."

Now Megan understood what Marla had seen the moment she'd told her about Brian Elkin: that once Steve had such a hold on this rich, weak man, he could not let go.

"He had me—the bastard had me empty my pockets. Took everything. Even the keys to the car. He told me he was leaving town but he'd be back. He—he didn't even try to make me think this was the end. That I'd be rid of him—didn't even try to make me think that any more." He had to break off to cough, but then he went on again. "He liked seeing me afraid. I knew I wouldn't have my money for months . . . and he'd be back. If he didn't get caught first. Didn't get us both caught. My God, he was going to take my car—going to run from the police in my car . . . The more scared I was the more he liked it. Only he never thought I'd go for him. I hit him and got him down. I had my hands on his throat and then the gun went off. I—"

But he had tried to talk too much. More blood bubbled on his lips and she heard that liquid soughing from his lungs. His eyes stared at her, but Megan sensed that he did not know who she was, could not remember what he had done to her. "I'm going for help," she said. "I'll get help for you." His eyelids flickered: that much he understood.

She struggled to her feet. Even before taking a step, she knew that the ankle was much worse now. She had to limp more slowly and carefully, and at every other step there was maddening pain. When she reached the bridge she could lean on the rail. Coming up to a stand of reeds, she tried grasping the taller, thicker stalks, but they only bent under her weight.

This was taking too long. It wasn't just the pain and her slow progress—she should have reached the bridge by now. There had been the light to guide her to the house, but there was nothing to guide her back to the bridge. Now the ground was soft and yielding and it cost more effort to lift her feet. She could see marsh grass and pools of water before her. She was in a bog. She had lost her way.

She stopped and raised her head. Through a place where the reeds were thin she could make out a far-off glow. The causeway. She staggered toward the light, in as straight a line as she could, not caring when she splashed through icy water.

She came to a steep rise. The embankment of the roadway. She started to climb it but her ankle would not bend. She got down on hands and knees and crawled to the top.

Here was the road, and on it a car. She had not heard it in the wind, but its bright red taillights were not far away. Her weakness screamed at her to snatch at this chance of help before it got away. Her hand closed on the butt of the flashlight in her pocket.

But the car was not moving. Megan let go the flashlight and held still, waiting, watching.

Abruptly the interior light came on. The door was swinging open. She saw Marla's white shirt and the dark shape of her head. She was trying to get out of the car. There was a blurred movement: Scapro lunging across the seat to pull the door shut. The light went out.

Megan waited for the taillights to dim as he took his foot off the brake, to grow smaller as he drove toward the causeway. But the car did not move.

She scrambled backward down the slope. Fear was at her again and she longed to run but could not. She could only hobble back through the mire as slowly as she had come. At last the ground began to rise, the footing to grow firmer. Even the slight incline made her go down on hands and knees.

When she raised her head, she could see the far-off lights of the village. She was at the edge of the sandy reach. She looked into the darkness to her right. She could not see the footbridge, but it had to be there. She struggled to her feet and limped toward it.

At last the darkness yielded up the boardwalk and the thin railing to her eyes. The rail was almost within reach. She took a last lunging step and grabbed it with both hands.

Hand over hand she began to pull herself across the bridge. The wind was behind her now, pushing her along. But now her hands and the spar of wood to which they clung turned pale and distinct. Twin shadows sprang from her feet and lengthened as if fleeing from her.

Then she heard the noise of the car behind her. She swung round and brilliant headlights dazzled her. The car stopped at the end of the bridge. There was a flash behind the lights and a snap like a bough breaking. Megan flinched. It took her a moment to understand that the bullet had not hit her. She turned and ran.

Her left leg buckled beneath her and she fell full-length. She got to her knees and knew she could get no further. Distinctly she heard Marla's voice crying out, "Let her go, Steve! Let her go!"

The car door slammed. She turned and looked into the lights. They flickered as Scapro ran in front of them. He was going to get close enough to make sure of his aim. She looked at the slick sand of the reach below. She could not jump, could not get out of the light in time. Her thoughts stopped.

The lights were gone. Megan stood blinking into darkness. She could see nothing at all. And from out of the darkness she heard Scapro shout "Marla!" It was a howl of rage and bafflement. For Marla, left alone in the car, had switched off the headlights.

Megan got off her knees, shifted to a crouch with her good leg under her. She could not hear or see Scapro, but the rickety planks of the bridge shifted a little as he moved. He wasn't going back. He was coming to get her. Without thinking, she knew what to do. She took the flashlight from her pocket. Cocking her arm back, she held its long barrel like a javelin, thumb poised on the switch. She would see him against the sky a moment before he saw her against the bridge.

She could hear only the wind. The bridge rocked beneath her. He was close.

The dark indistinct shape loomed up against the clouds. Now. She flicked on the flashlight. For an instant she saw his face in the brilliant spot of light, the eyes screwed shut and teeth bared, the hand that held the gun probing vainly in front of him. She sprang. Her arm whipped over her shoulder and drove the light into his face.

She fell to the planks, sprawling, rolling. Her legs kicked out into emptiness. She swung them back onto the bridge. When she could raise her head and look back, Scapro was gone. The light was gone—the impact had jarred it from her hand. She dragged herself to the edge of the bridge.

It took time for her eyes to adjust to the dark again, and then she could make out the pale smudges of his face and hands. He was lying in the sand below her, and he was still.

She rolled over, away from him. She did not try to get up, but began to drag herself over the rough planks on elbows and knees. Eventually she could hear the sound of the car's idling engine. She called out to Marla.

For a moment she thought that the girl had run away yet again. But then the bridge rocked a little, and in a moment Marla was kneeling beside her. Megan turned her head. She could see Marla's eyes, wide and shining, staring straight ahead. She expected Steve Scapro to rear up out of the darkness and punish her for what she had done.

"I hit him hard," Megan told her. "He's not coming back."

5

Megan woke up abruptly. It was like the beginning of a movie, the big screen filling with light in the dark room. But the image was blurred and far away. She was someplace bright and noisy, and there was someone by her bed. A hospital, she thought. She remembered now that they had taken her to a hospital last night. Last night? She had no idea what time it was now. Her head was cloudy with drugs. She did not mind. She was happy. She felt like a child who was sick, but not too sick. Nothing would be expected of her. She was going to be pampered and looked after.

Her attention returned unhurriedly to the figure beside the bed. Her eyes were open, so the person knew that she was awake. It might be someone who was going to ask her questions. There had been so many people asking her questions, last night or whenever it was. Ugly thoughts came into her mind, but she turned them away. It was wonderfully easy to turn them away. Instead, she considered whether this person might be Paul. She swallowed and spoke his name.

It was he. He drew nearer and said, "Yes, love."

She knew she was in a hospital then. Paul had never been one for endearments. She said, "What hospital is this?"

"Stamford. You're back home."

"Oh." Her eyes were coming into focus, and her mind was clearing. The same ugly thoughts came back at her. She felt as if only a few minutes had passed since she had been on the bridge in the dark. She was afraid, as she had not been afraid then. "Is he here? Is he anywhere near me?"

Paul understood. "No. Nowhere near. He's in a hospital in New York. Various jurisdictions are fighting over who gets him first."

Megan nodded and relaxed. But now that she had started she had another question to ask. It was like trying to catch a feather that floated away when her hands, reaching for it, stirred the air. She waited for it to settle. "You're not in jail. I was so afraid you'd be in jail."

"I'm free on my own recognizance. It was tense for a while there, and they dragged up something or other to charge me with, but I think it will blow over. Stephanie's in a very good mood. She's delighted to have Brian Elkin. He can hardly talk yet, but he's making statements anyway. He's going to be great in court. It's what he's been waiting his whole life for. An audience that has to listen to him, and a lawyer to tell them why they ought to feel sorry for him. The trial and appeals will drag on so long he'll forget he's going to jail at the end."

Megan said, "I'll be going to jail."

"No."

"Tell me the truth, Paul."

"All right. We have every reason to hope not. We have every reason to hope for a suspended sentence and a period of probation." He paused for a moment. "But they're going to make that deal with you because they want your testimony against Elkin and Scapro. You're going to have to spend a lot of time in interview rooms and courtrooms over the next months. A lot of lawyers will take a crack at you. You're in for a hard time."

She tried to raise her head and turn toward him, but the movement made her too dizzy. There was something she had to say, something crucial and unpleasant. She wished that she could think clearly.

"Listen, Paul. I want that. I want it all to be dragged out and repeated until everyone is bored with hearing it. I want to say what I did, over and over. Maybe then I can get rid of it." She tried again to raise her head. "You can't understand that, can you? To you it's just deals being made, and lawyers taking cracks."

"That's all there is, Meg." She heard a touch of that old loftiness and asperity in his voice. "You don't know the nuts and bolts of the law the way I do."

"You haven't gone through what I've gone through."

A pause, and then Paul said, "No, I haven't."

"So you don't know. There's more to it than that." She wanted to explain, but the words kept slipping away. "There's more to it."

"All right. I'll take your word for that."

"Lean over me, will you? I want to see you."

His face slid into view. He was very near, but her vision was blurring again. "Paul, I'm not going to let go of you, and that means you're going to get dragged through all this with me."

"It's my disaster too, you know. I had a hand in it."

The interruption threw her off the track. "I mean . . . I mean . . . there are going to be times when you wish you'd never set eyes on me."

"I'll have to take your word for that, too." She could not see him very well, but she could tell that he was smiling. "Will I have many times like that?"

She thought a moment. "No, not many."

The sun-filled clouds were setting over her mind now. She wanted to take Paul's hand before she drifted away. She started to reach out to him.

"Other hand," he said.

"Am I handcuffed to the bed?"

He chuckled. "No, of course not. But you cut that hand badly and it's infected. It's all bandaged up."

"Oh." She lifted her other hand across her body so that Paul could take it. "I can't stay awake. But even if I drop off, hold onto me, okay?"

"I will. Go to sleep. They've got you drugged to the gills because of your ankle."

"My ankle. Yes." It did not hurt at all now, but she knew that it was going to. She said, in a voice that was slow and thick, "It's going to be okay? Isn't it?"

"Yes."

"Do you love me?"

"Yes."

She didn't talk any more. She gripped his hand and let sleep take her.